GRAIL QUEST

THE
CAMELOT
SPELL

◆ BOOK ONE ◆

GRAIL QUEST

THE
CAMELOT
SPELL

LAURA ANNE GILMAN

HARPERCOLLINS*PUBLISHERS*
A PARACHUTE PRESS BOOK

Many thanks to Anne Kelleher for her help.

Library of Congress Cataloging-in-Publication Data
Gilman, Laura Anne.
  The Camelot spell / Laura Anne Gilman. — 1st ed.
    p. cm. — (Grail quest ; 1)
  Summary: Three teenagers living in Camelot are forced to undertake a
dangerous mission when King Arthur's court falls under a mysterious enchant-
ment on the eve of the quest for the Holy Grail.
  ISBN-10: 0-06-077279-4 (trade bdg.) — ISBN-13: 978-0-06-077279-6
(trade bdg.)
  ISBN-10: 0-06-077280-8 (lib. bdg.) — ISBN-13: 978-0-06-077280-2 (lib. bdg.)
  [1. Knights and knighthood—Fiction. 2. Arthur, King—Fiction. 3. Middle
Ages—Fiction. 4. Magic—Fiction.] I. Title. II. Series.
PZ7.G43325Cam 2006
[Fic] — dc22
                                                                2005008527

1 2 3 4 5 6 7 8 9 10

First Edition

For Daniel and Evan Klein

PROLOGUE

"This is such a remarkably bad idea. There's no possible way it will work. It's no wonder I thought of it."

The people of Camelot were well accustomed to seeing—and hearing—Merlin wandering the halls at odd hours, muttering to himself. And so they passed him by with no more than a dutiful curtsey or nod of the head. You didn't want to distract the king's most famous and dangerous advisor, but neither did you want to risk his anger.

He hadn't turned anyone into a rat in years. But you never knew . . . with enchanters.

"The question is," Merlin went on, walking down a long hallway that led from his tower to the main part of the castle, "was I under a spell when I thought of it, or was I just being particularly stupid that day?"

One of the many drawbacks of living backward in time, as he did: You knew what you had done because you saw the results of it, but unless you left yourself careful notes—something Merlin always forgot to do—you had no idea *why* you had done it. Confusing. But then so much of his life, aside from the parts that were impossible, was confusing. One simply got used to it after a while.

Merlin turned a corner and found himself in an antechamber in the main building. Camelot was one of those palaces where every place you wanted to be always seemed to be the farthest spot from where you were—except this room. This room was in the heart of the castle. This room was, in many ways, the soul of Camelot.

He commanded the great wooden doors in front of him to open, using the language of magic he had learned years before he knew who he was or what his role in King Arthur's life would be.

The magic worked at his command, as it always did. The heavy, metal locks on the doors slid open without anyone touching them, allowing Merlin access into the Room. There was a smaller door set into the great doors that was used by servants and pages to enter and leave during council sessions without disturbing those inside. But Merlin was in a mood today and felt no need to use a servants' entrance. Besides, the enchanter was taller than most in Camelot and he had no desire to bend over almost double to use the smaller door. Servants' trousers and tunics might look fine when ducking and scraping; the robes of an enchanter did not.

The Room was the official Council Room, but nobody called it that. If anyone in all of Camelot mentioned "the Room," everyone knew what they were talking about. This was the room where King Arthur—the warlord of Britain, the uniter of the tribes against the invaders from Rome—held counsel with his most favored, most wise knights, all of them seated around the great council table.

The thought was enough to make the ancient enchanter give a disdainful snort as he walked into the Room. Then he sneezed.

"Someone's forgotten to clean in here again," he muttered, drawing his robes aside as he walked through the Room, his soft leather shoes kicking up a faint cloud of dust. The tapestries on the stone walls were dulled, and the floor itself—was that a half-gnawed bone on the floor? Merlin rolled his eyes in an overly dramatic fashion. Some of the knights King Arthur gathered around himself were great fighters, yes, and occasionally one of them had a logical thought in his head, but their manners were deplorable. The greatest of England, pffagh. He made a noise of disgust.

And this newest idea of the king's, this Quest for the Holy Grail . . . pffagh again. The last thing King Arthur needed was to send his men haring about on some foolishness when he should be keeping them close at hand. But one might as well talk to a horse as Arthur once the boy had an idea stuck in his head.

Perhaps it was not entirely madness. The Grail, beyond its significance as a holy relic, was an object of true power with the weight of a thousand years of history behind it. Although it pained Merlin to admit it, there were things his magic could not accomplish for King Arthur; places where neither magic nor warriors swayed minds or hearts. But this Grail—the Christians' Holy Grail—might indeed be the answer to that.

And if Arthur wanted the Grail for more than simply political reasons; a matter of religion per-haps—well, each man must choose his own God, as he sees fit. So long as he keeps his feet firmly on this earth, while he lives on it.

Despite the dust on the floor, the Table itself gleamed, the entire surface made from a single great oak Arthur himself had chosen. He came up with some astonishingly stupid ideas, yes, but even Merlin had to admit that the Table was a good one. A round table, where none might feel greater or lesser than any other? A table where any man might sit next to his king and lean over to give him counsel? Yes, a good idea. An excellent idea, cementing the petty war-leaders and chieftains to the warrior-king who united them. Though at times such conviviality led men into thinking that they were all equal, and they were not. Some were greater fools than the others.

Speaking of which . . .

"You, Gerard," the enchanter snapped. "Tell someone to clean in here! I don't care if it is winter and they're bored out of their small skulls. Arthur cannot call his knights to order when they can't speak for coughing."

He grinned at the startled young creature who appeared in front of him. The boy had been hiding behind one of the tapestries that lined the chamber—the one that showed Arthur taking his sword Excalibur from the stone in order to prove his lineage. The boy had been snooping where he shouldn't have been, obviously, and hid when he heard Merlin come in. Now he stared at the enchanter, his eyes open wide.

"There's no magic to knowing your name, boy." Well, all right, *some* magic. How else could he tell the little beasts that passed for pages and squires apart? "As for finding you . . . you left a trail in the dust. And you're the only one of your pack who would be in here, touching and nosing where you've no right to be. No, no apologies. I admire that sort of behavior. When you've got power, then you can play by the rules. Until then, make do with whatever you can find or ferret out."

"That's not—" Gerard started, suddenly realizing who he was arguing with.

"Not right? Not knightly behavior? Maybe. Maybe not." Merlin bent forward and looked at the boy closely. The squire's blond hair had been cut short, the better to fit under a helm, and his big blue eyes held something familiar in them. . . .

"Right. Kay's nephew, the one who's been fostered to Rheynold?" Fostering was the current popular practice of sending your boy-children, when they reached a certain age, to be raised in the household of another knight who could train them without letting ties of blood or affection interfere.

Rheynold didn't take many squires, but when the king's own foster brother asks . . .

Without waiting for the squire to respond, the enchanter nodded his head, his own eyes dark and sharp above an eagle's beak of a nose. "You've impressed me, boy, although cursed if I can remember how, since it hasn't happened yet. Keep up with it, keep up with it! And mind you tell those useless wretches to dust in here!"

* * *

Gerard watched the tall, slender form of the wizard circle the Round Table, waving his hands and still talking until he came to Arthur's chair. Carved out of a dark polished wood, it was half as large as the other chairs that Gerard had—carefully, cautiously—been sitting in, but otherwise looked the same as all the others, with straight backs and uncomfortable seats. Gerard knew from having served during council sessions that some of the knights brought cushions with them but still found the great chairs uncomfortable. Gerard didn't care. He wanted to sit at the Table so badly he could taste it. That was what was important: to be one of King Arthur's trusted companions, a knight proven in valor and honor.

"As it was done, so let it be done. There."

Gerard looked up again to see Merlin scattering a strange, shiny powder over Arthur's chair, then dusting his hands off as though to get rid of the last flakes. "Not that it does any good, but it might have been far worse without it. Idiot warlords, always having something to prove. And worse when there's a woman involved, as I should well have learned by now. Especially during the winter. Too many minstrels whining on about courtly love. Pffagh. None of this 'longing from afar' nonsense for me. You want something? Go after it. Don't sit around and moon because you're too noble to get your hands muddy."

Merlin noticed Gerard staring at him. "What, you still here? Go, shoo. Go!"

Gerard didn't wait to be told a third time, taking to his heels and leaving the enchanter to whatever he was doing. Sir Rheynold would be furious if he knew Gerard had been lingering in the Council Room where he was not supposed to be.

"Although," a little voice that sounded a lot like his own said to him, "I wasn't exactly alone. Merlin was there. And *he* didn't scold me."

"Merlin is insane," another voice in his head countered, this one sounding a great deal like Sir

Bors, a companion of his foster father, Sir Kay, and the knight who taught the squires their lessons. "Useful, but insane."

And with that voice, the squire could not disagree.

*   *   *

In the room which held the great Round Table of King Arthur, the enchanter named Merlin looked at his handiwork, but his mind was preoccupied with the young boy who had just fled.

"Insane, yes," he agreed with the voice in Gerard's head. "But oh, so useful!" Now if Merlin could only remember what it was that he knew about this boy, and what role he would play in all that was going to happen.

Too much happening, the enchanter decided finally. Too many intersections, too many potential outcomes. Too many enemies waiting to strike. Magic could only look so far into the future—and then it all became chaos.

"Ah well, old man," he said to himself, chuckling. "That's half the point, isn't it? Think how boring it would be if everyone knew where they were going all the time."

ONE

"This entire castle has gone mad!"

Gerard instinctively ducked out of the way as the chief cook sent his assistants into motion with a wave of one muscled arm, flinging flour-dust over everyone within range. The spring morning was warm, and thrice so down here, where the ovens were burning hot and flour stuck to sweaty skin and dampened tunics and aprons. His face already perspiring, the squire hung close to the doorway, mentally cursing his master for sending him down to the kitchens today of all days.

"It's the Quest," one of the under-bakers ventured from where they huddled near the great brick ovens of Camelot's kitchen.

The cook glowered at the boy who'd spoken. "Of course it's the Quest! Everything has been *the Quest*

10

for months now! And I, for one, will be glad when they're all gone and out of my hair"—Gerard, along with everyone else in the kitchen, refrained from pointing out that Cook had no hair—"and we can get back to living like civilized folk!" He caught sight of Gerard by the door and pointed one over-sized, flour-covered hand at him. "You. What are you doing here?"

The squire swallowed hard, reminding himself that in his fourteen years of life, he had faced much worse than Cook's temper. Well, faced some things *almost* as bad, anyway. "Message from my master, Sir Rheynold, about—"

"About that bird of his, I'll wager, no?" Cook was a fearsome-looking mountain of a man at the best of times. But when he smiled, even brave knights took a step back. "Tell your master the fowl arrived safely and will be a masterpiece when we're done with it. Rest easy."

Gerard personally hated the taste of peacock, especially when the outer layer of flesh was stuffed with roasted pigeon the way his master enjoyed it, but he knew better than to say so. It was not his place, as a mere squire, to speak anything but good of his master's choices. Especially when the dish was one the king was also reported to enjoy, and Sir Rheynold was currying favor by arranging for the banquet tonight.

All the knights did it, one way or another, with presents or sweet words or brave actions dedicated to the king and his queen. Arthur was an easygoing man, for a king, but he wore the crown, and the crown had the power. Gerard had lived in Camelot for six years now under Sir Rheynold's fosterage, and he thought he understood how things went. Power was to be catered to, and you had to establish your own power in turn. Or, in Gerard's case, maintain the power of the man who sheltered and trained him. That was the way of the world.

Nodding his head to give the right amount of respect due to a servant of Cook's ability and reputation, Gerard said, "I'll tell Sir Rheynold of your assurances. I am sure he thanks you for your attention to this offering."

Message delivered, he turned to escape the heat and chaos of the kitchen. He should have gone directly back to his master's rooms up in the east wing of the castle to see what else might be required of him. But Cook had not been exaggerating about the energy that was filling Camelot. Two months prior, Arthur had announced a Quest. It had come to him in a dream, he said. A great Quest, blessed by God, to search out and find the Holy Grail brought to this island by Joseph of Arimathea from the Holy Land and then lost for centuries after his death.

The Knights of the Round Table would find it. Restore it. Bring it back to Camelot, where it would be the fitting symbol of Arthur's kingship, alongside his sword Excalibur. It would be a glorious, wonderful thing.

For the past week, men had been riding to Camelot to speak with Arthur and explain why they should be honored with a place on this Quest. At the banquet tonight, Arthur himself would proclaim the names of the knights who would ride out on this Quest of his. The entire castle *was* mad from it; so much so that anyone caught unoccupied was sure to be put to work.

Gerard never shirked from work . . . but he saw no reason to look for it, either. Especially, he admitted reluctantly to himself, since the Quest had completely overlooked him. Not that he, a mere squire, would have been allowed to take part, but he was no more immune to the dreams than any other. To be the one who found the legendary Holy Grail, who brought it home to Arthur's hands and reaped the praise and rewards such a treasure must bring . . .

"But first you'd have to be there to find it. And that's not going to happen now, is it?" he told himself, moving down the narrow side-halls that were used only by servants and the occasional page or squire in a hurry. No, it wouldn't be he who found the Grail, even if he had been allowed to go along on the search. One of the knights would find it. Most likely Lancelot, who was the perfect knight, brave and noble and kind even to the clumsiest of pages, although his face was not handsome. Or Gawain, whom everyone called "the Pure." No, not a lowly squire, no matter how noble his bloodlines might be.

A page, his young face flushed with exertion, hurried toward him with half a dozen parchments under one arm. "Gerard, Pickleface is looking for you!"

"Drat it," Gerard muttered, waving his thanks to the younger boy. If Pickleface—Master Balin, so-called because of the sourness of his expression—was looking for him, it could only be bad. As a squire, Gerard was supposed to be above any duties the page-master might give him, but explaining that to this adult would earn him a sound boxing on the ears and he'd *still* have to do whatever Balin had in mind.

On a whim, Gerard took the left-hand hallway instead of the right, and eased open the door in the stone wall to find himself in the courtyard opposite from the stable.

He crossed the courtyard quickly, then let himself into the stable. The cool shade inside the wooden structure was a relief after the heat of the kitchen. He blinked and let his eyes adjust. It seemed quiet enough, despite so many knights having their horses stabled there. More than fifty had come to Camelot. Of them, twenty-seven knights total, plus their squires fortunate enough to travel with them, would soon set off on the Quest. No more and no less, Arthur had decreed: Nine times three, for a number that was pleasing to him. The knights would be dependent upon themselves, not what they could bring with them, and so all would begin the Quest as equals.

"Some more equal than others," Gerard said to himself, reaching up to stroke the neck of his master's beast, a roan gelding with a surprisingly sweet disposition, despite a wicked-looking eye. "A good horse will trump a wise man every day," he murmured into the horse's ear, quoting something his master often said—especially when Gerard's actions or words failed to please him.

"Here now, away from him!"

Gerard turned, astonished. A stable boy stood not a foot from him, hands fisted at his hips, a scowl on his face. He wore dark trousers and a shirt made of a rough homespun and streaked with sweat and dirt. Shaggy black hair fell over his forehead and into his eyes, for all the world like a pony's forelock.

"Away from the horse," the boy repeated slowly, as though speaking to a dullard who could not be expected to understand his words. In the dim light, the boy was unable to see Gerard's tunic, which was marked in the upper corner with his master's colors, proclaiming him a member of that knight's household.

On a normal day, Gerard would have remembered the manners expected of him, and the responsibility lectured into him from his first hour with Sir Rheynold. On a normal day, he would have informed the stable boy that he was squire to the man to whom this horse belonged, and thus within rights to touch such an expensive beast. On a normal day, he would even have thanked the boy for keeping such good watch, above and beyond his duties to shovel and polish.

But it wasn't a normal day. And it certainly wasn't

a good day, considering that he had been up and running errands since dawn as though he were still a page. It rankled the competent squire, emphasizing the fact that he wasn't considered man enough to go on the Quest. And Gerard suddenly very much wanted someone other than himself to share his unhappiness. A stable boy, someone so low in Camelot's pecking order as to be almost invisible, was perfect.

"Begone, sirrah," Gerard said, drawing himself up to his proud height. Although he hadn't reached his full growth yet, he looked far more imposing than the scrawny boy before him. "I'll do what I please, as I please, with my horseflesh." And the horse *was* his, in a way. That was part of the oath Sir Rheynold made in return for his services. To teach and to care for Gerard, and to give to him as if he were the man's own son.

"Sure," the other boy said scornfully. "You've the look of the d'Abmonts, that's certain."

Gerard flushed. Sir Rheynold d'Abmont was a huge bear of a man, ruddy-faced and red-haired; nothing at all like his own more fair and slender form.

"I am his squire, Gerard of Abmont." He might

have claimed his family name—he was of the bloodline of Sir Kay, the foster brother of the king himself—but that was bragging, and he had done nothing to earn it save be born. His place in the Abmont household he had *earned*.

The stable boy snorted, sounding a great deal like a horse himself. "It wouldn't matter if you're the king's own nephew; you're not touching the beasts in my care."

"Your care?" Gerard could feel himself spluttering, outraged to be dismissed like that. "Yours? You dung-smeared, rear-faced, snot-nosed . . . peasant!"

As easily as that, they were down on the straw-strewn ground between the wooden stalls, wrestling to get the best hold on the other. Gerard thought he had the upper hand, managing to land a solid elbow into the other boy's face. But the stable boy was agile, slipping from his grasp again and again. He got in a blow with the heel of his hand first to Gerard's jaw and then solidly into his nose.

Gerard tasted blood in the back of his throat and spat straw out of his mouth as they rolled, the sound of nervous horses snorting and shifting in the stalls around them.

"Enough!"

A hand reached down and grasped Gerard by the collar of his shirt, lifted him off the other boy, and tossed him onto his backside. It soothed the blow only slightly to see the stable boy treated in the same manner. But that sense of justice faded when he recognized the newcomer.

Sir Lancelot, his ugly-handsome face set in lines of absolute exasperation, glared down at them.

"Gerard, for the love of God, what *were* you thinking—assuming you were thinking at all . . . I expect far better behavior of you than to be scuffling about like an ill-bred child."

Gerard's complexion flushed again and he bit his tongue to keep from responding like the sulky child Sir Lancelot accused him of being. A perfect day: first running errands like a mere page, and now this.

He knew full well that fighting with a stable boy was not acceptable behavior for a squire who was almost ready to be considered for knighting. He knew that and had done it anyway. And in front of Lancelot! The respectable man was everything that Gerard hoped someday to be—a great warrior and Arthur's most trusted knight. Or at least he had been until recently. Lancelot spent more time away from Camelot now, almost as though he were avoiding the place.

The thought of having disappointed the most famous Knight of the Round Table was more bitter than any scolding or punishment he might receive. But still—Gerard fought down the anger that rose in his throat—it wasn't fair! He had been provoked!

"And you, Newt. Thirteen's old enough to leave off childish ways." Lancelot looked down at the stable boy, who had scrambled to his feet, and cuffed him across one ear. "I despair of ever teaching you manners."

Newt grinned up at the knight and wiped his nose with the back of his hand. "Maybe I'm no gallant, but I speak the truth, Lance. You know that."

Gerard almost choked on his outrage then, that this . . . *nothing* dared use the king's own nickname for the greatest knight in all Camelot. But Lancelot didn't seem to mind. "Back to work, you. And Gerard, go clean yourself. The banquet will begin soon and I'll not have you disgracing your master further by appearing with straw in your hair as well as a bloodied nose."

Gerard got to his feet, brushing straw out of his hair and off his backside.

"Go on," Newt said, mimicking Lancelot's tone perfectly. "Must be tidy for the castle."

"Newt!" Another crack across the ear, this one harder. But not hard enough to suit Gerard.

The squire left, shooting a sharp look at Newt as he went. Scolded like a puppy, and that boy got away with such familiarity!

"It's not fair," Gerard muttered to himself, kicking at a clod of dirt and watching it skitter across the stones of the courtyard.

"It rarely is," Lancelot said from behind him. Gerard jumped, startled. He had been so wrapped up in his own misery, he hadn't heard the knight catch up to him. The knight's eyes were kind with sympathy. "Life, that is. But you'll find your way around it," Lancelot continued, matching himself to Gerard's slower pace. "Or, if you don't, it will be a failure of your own, not your birth or education, neither of which Newt has. Keep that in mind, young Gerard. We who have the benefit of our station in this world must never forget it, even in the face of provocation."

Gerard thought about that for a few steps. Sir Kay had said that honesty was a knight's best virtue (even if that did make Merlin laugh).

"I was angry," the squire said finally. "Not at him, I mean. When I went in there. And he was . . ."

"There?" Lancelot asked.

"Annoying."

"That he is," Lancelot agreed with a laugh. "Second only to his skill with horses. And you saw him as the first available target, didn't you?"

Gerard opened his mouth to deny it, then shrugged.

"It happens," Lancelot said. "Yes, even to me. You should hear some of the arguments Merlin and I have had. And yes, I know what sort of an idiot that makes me, to quarrel with an enchanter." Lancelot smiled briefly. "Fortunately, Arthur has thus far kept him from turning me into a particularly pink-eyed rat."

Gerard felt his lips turn up in a smile at the thought of Lancelot as a rat, but the sense of unfairness still burned inside him. There was no way Lancelot could understand, not really. He *had* everything he wanted.

Then Gerard looked sideways at Lancelot, noting the exhaustion in the knight's face and remembering the weeks and months he spent away from Camelot. Some said he was on the king's secret orders. Some claimed he was chasing a woman. Others merely narrowed their eyes, putting a finger to their lips and looking wise. Whatever his reasons, it seemed that only the Grail Quest could bring Lancelot home, looking even sadder than he had when he left.

Maybe even Sir Lancelot didn't get everything he wanted. Not all the time. It was something to think about.

"And off you go," the knight said as they reached the inner wall of the castle, not the door Gerard had used earlier, but a wooden gate that led to the east wing of the castle, where the King's guests were housed. "Scurry, and I won't have to make any excuses for you with the most fearsome Gracelan."

Since everyone knew that the chatelaine, the woman who oversaw the daily keeping of Camelot, was sweet on Lancelot, Gerard wasn't too frightened of the threat. Lancelot would avoid her the way squires avoided Sir Bors.

Shaking his head at what a strange, confusing day it had already been, Gerard hurried across the common area and up the narrow stone staircase and headed for his own pallet in his master's room. If the bells hadn't rung yet, he would still have time to wash up before dinner, but not much.

* * *

Twenty minutes later, his hair slicked back, the blood, straw, and mud washed from his skin, and the worst of his bruises treated with salve, Gerard skidded to a stop outside the great carved doors of the Feasting Hall. Taking a deep breath, he nodded to the guards standing on either side, and stepped inside.

Chaos immediately engulfed him, and a harried-looking server shoved a platter of pies into his arms and pushed him toward the rows of trestle tables set up along the far wall.

"And don't be slow about it!"

The hall itself, so huge and daunting to Gerard when he first came to Camelot as a page, was now simply huge. It was difficult to feel daunted when you were being run off your feet.

But tonight, with all the banners of the knights in residence hung on the walls, it seemed even more impressive somehow; the colors fighting with the sounds and smells for his attention. This was the largest feast Gerard had ever seen. The addition of the squires to the usual serving pages was barely enough to keep everything running.

There were more than a dozen long, wooden tables set up, each one crammed with as many honored guests as could fit on the carved wooden benches, and each table was piled with plates and knives and goblets. The walls rose four man-heights to a beamed ceiling that curved in such a way as to swallow much of the noise rising from the tables. The tapestries and banners on the walls muffled even more, but it was still impossibly noisy.

Despite that, every page and squire was expected to hear every word said to them, and respond promptly and courteously with the speaker's correct name and title.

Gerard hoisted his tray and set to work, dodging another page and almost colliding with a serving maid before he found the rhythm. Making his way carefully among the other servers, and darting around the minstrels and players who used the space in front of the tables to perform, Gerard was exhausted within an hour. And rumor had it this feast would go on until well after midnight!

"Boy, sit a moment."

The voice cutting through the babble was familiar and Gerard didn't need to be told twice. He knelt by his master's side, resting one elbow on the edge of the table. Sir Rheynold was highly placed, as befitted one of Arthur's oldest followers, down somewhat from the formality of the high table where Arthur and his queen sat, but well above the great silver salt dish. Below the salt, the unproven knights and commoners worked on their food, and the younger, less-schooled pages served them.

"They've got you all going in every direction save down," Sir Rheynold said, passing Gerard a sip from the knight's own goblet. The ale was cool and thick, and went down smooth.

"Everyone's a bit on nerves," Gerard agreed, enjoying the rest as much as the drink. Some knights wanted their squires to be seen and not heard—and seen only when needed—but Sir Rheynold had always been a good and patient teacher; he welcomed Gerard's questions and observations.

"Tcha." Rheynold shook his head and stroked the bristles of his beard with an index finger. "This Quest of Arthur's . . . it's a grand idea, to be sure. A fine noble cause to get all the hotheads out of the castle and doing something useful for a change. The Grail will help cement Arthur's hold outside of the Isle, where people have not met him or are leery of the power Merlin and his magic might have over him. Those who don't trust Arthur may yet trust the man who holds the Grail."

"Why?" Gerard asked, not wanting to seem ignorant but genuinely curious.

"The Grail is more than an object, Gerard. It is a symbol. And in these times—in all times—men respond well to symbols. Especially when the symbol is in the possession of a strong leader." The old knight took back his goblet and swallowed a heavy mouthful. "But I'm glad to be out of it, I am. Quests and cavalcades . . . they're nasty things for a man my age. Leave it to the young and bold."

I'm young and bold, Gerard thought but didn't say. It would have done him no good. Rheynold was a fair master. But even he would not take well to what could be considered insolence from one of his charges.

"Psssst!" A piercing whisper came from another squire standing a few feet away, just far enough to be polite. He was gesturing urgently and his expression indicated the need for haste.

Rheynold looked up, a smile on his age-lined face. "Go on, boy. They're in need of you again."

Gerard ducked his head and got back to his feet, tugging at his fancy tunic so that it hung properly, the gold and silver thread of Arthur's crest displayed proudly. It felt strange to be wearing the king's livery instead of Sir Rheynold's, but Gracelan wanted all the servers to look the same tonight to keep confusion to a minimum. If Gerard spilled anything on this, he thought bleakly, the washerwomen would tear strips off his hide.

"Where to now?" he asked Mak, the squire who had signaled him.

"Cook's ready to bring out the soltetie—wants us to usher it in."

The soltetie was a "disguised" dish, in this case a huge pig roasted and decorated with feathers and antlers to appear like some fanciful beast. Cook typically used adult servants to bear the heaviest dishes, but servants weren't grand enough for this banquet.

"I don't suppose Cook would believe I've an old battle wound keeping me from lifting anything heavier than a stuffed duck?" Gerard said hopefully.

"A battle wound? That's a good one. What, did the king's fool plant an arrow in your backside?"

Gerard aimed a mock cuff at Mak's head. The other squire ducked it easily, making a disgusting face at him after first making sure no adults were watching.

"Perhaps if you carry your share gallantly, the king will demand you join the Quest for him personally to return the Grail to civilized hands."

"Can you imagine it," Gerard began, forgetting everything else to return to his favorite topic. "To be a part of . . . to actually lay hands on the Grail itself? They say it's magical, that it can heal, that it can grant your heart's dearest wish. . . ."

"Will it make you better at your sword drills? That would be miracle indeed!"

"Oh, for heaven's sake." A girl's voice, light and pleasant in tone, if not in the words, intruded into their conversation. "Grail this, Grail that. None of you has a lick of sense about it."

Gerard made an irritated face at Mak, but smoothed it out before turning to face the newcomer. Ailis might be only a girl, and a servant at that, but she had come to Camelot after the battle of Mount Agned, where both her parents died. Everyone knew that the queen looked after the orphans of that battle as if, some whispered unkindly, they were the children she had never been able to give the king. And those whom Guinevere favored had a certain kind of protection, in that everyone took care to please the queen. To anger the queen was to risk Arthur's wrath as well.

Gerard and Ailis had both come to Camelot as tearful eight-year-olds the same week, and there was a bond of sorts in that. (Even if neither would ever

29

admit that one of them had gotten lost in the winding stone-and-wood hallways of the castle, and had to be led out, in tears, by the other.) Gerard would take that secret to his grave. Ailis might only be a servant-girl, but her parents had been honest landholders who died for their king. And she was a good sort, for a girl.

"What do you mean?" Mak demanded. "How are we not sensible? I'd say we're being plenty sensible—can't go on a Quest without planning, and lots of it!"

Ailis had pretty brown eyes that could practically sparkle with laughter, but right now they looked dark and worried. "The Grail is not to be won, is it? It's a thing that's given." She tugged at the end of her braid, which was dark red and long enough to coil around her shoulder and hang almost down to her elbow. "You can't just go off and search and take it, no matter how shining your armor or fancy your horse, or full your heart with Glory-to-King."

"And pray tell: Who gives it, then?" Mak scoffed.

"I don't know," Ailis admitted, looking troubled by the question. "But someone more than a knight."

"You know nothing about it." Gerard couldn't believe that she was dismissing all the knights that easily. Lancelot himself was on this Quest! It was all anyone had talked about for months!

"Nor does any of us," Ailis pointed out. "Everything we've heard so far . . . it's just legend. And myth. But all the stories say that the one who holds it cannot be defeated on this earth."

"All the more reason for Arthur to hold it," Gerard said.

"But what if we're not the ones meant to find it? Might it not be better for it to stay lost?" Ailis suggested.

Mak was scornful. "You're a servant. What do you know about any of this?"

Ailis gulped, her cheeks going pale and then flaming red with shame. "Is that what you think? That a servant can't know any better?"

On another day, Gerard might have tried to smooth things over, as he so often did when Ailis spoke her mind in front of his fellow squires. But he was still upset at the stable boy's actions, and her dismissal of his heroes rankled him. "You're a girl," he said instead. "Maybe that's why—"

"Oh!" Ailis looked as though she'd like to smack them both, but settled for a parting shot before she turned away. "Two of a kind, you are; overfull of yourselves and your positions—such as they are, as neither of you is actually being taken along on this grand Quest."

They both winced as the bolt struck home.

"Ailis, I . . ." Gerard began awkwardly.

"Oh, go on, they're calling you," Ailis said, spotting a commotion near the main door. "Hurry!"

* * *

Ailis watched the two boys move across the crowded floor to where one of the under-cooks was waiting, and sighed in relief when they made it without further delay. She hated to see anyone get into trouble. Then, recalling her own duties, she lifted the refilled pitcher of spiced wine and made her way carefully back to where her ladies waited. At fourteen, Ailis was one of the youngest of the queen's servants, chosen for her quick eyes and steady hands. Unlike the pages and squires, she had only to serve wine and set out fresh napkins at this feast. But it took all her concentration to anticipate their needs without appearing to eavesdrop on them. Especially when they said such interesting—and gossipy—things.

"Do you not think Sir Gawain has the greatest chance? He is . . . very religious."

"So religious he will seek the Grail only in churches and monasteries," another woman at the table suggested, waving her bejeweled hands in dismissal. "If the Grail were there, it would have been found already."

Ailis kept her gaze lowered and her mouth shut as she refilled her lady's goblet and replaced stained napkins with new squares of cloth. It was one thing to argue with Mak and Gerard, despite their squire's rank. Responding to an adult was out of the question. No, she was a servant, and as such would never dare speak her mind to any of the court, not even if they asked her. That would lead to dismissal, and no matter that the queen had been known to smile upon her from time to time.

Someday soon, she knew, Mak and Gerard and the others would earn their spurs and go off to be knights in the service of the king, but she would still be here, serving at the castle. That was the fate of a landless, family-less orphan.

"Oh, stop feeling so sorry for yourself," she scolded herself quietly. A practical girl, Ailis knew it wasn't a bad life. Lonely? A little. But she was well treated and fed and cared for, and was learning skills that would be useful as she got older. She had a fine hand with her stitching. That might earn her a place as a seamstress, eventually, in the queen's cozy, comfortable solar. But . . .

"I want more than to be a seamstress or the mistress of the linens in some lord's manor house," she whispered fiercely to the food-stained napkins in her grasp. "I want . . . "

Her thought was interrupted by something odd. Her head lifted, like a doe scenting the air, and her young lips creased in a frown. The musicians . . . that was it. The musician playing the lute—his tune was off somehow. Not much, perhaps nothing most in the crowd would notice, but Ailis had a good ear as well as a pure singing voice, and music she knew well.

Ailis shrugged. Perhaps he had drunk too much mead. Or he was tired. They had been performing for hours now, and it was far more difficult work, she knew, than any observer would think. Either way, it was no concern of hers.

But still. Something was odd, now that she looked about her. It wasn't a specific thing, exactly— a smell that was off in the air, maybe, like wood smoke, only not as familiar or comforting as that. Movements were also off, slowed somehow, as though it were just a bit too much effort to carry on as usual.

Worried now, Ailis instinctively looked over her shoulder to check on the queen. Others might think the sun rose and set on King Arthur. He was the lion of the court indeed, but Ailis had long ago learned that Guinevere's moods set the temper of the castle, not Arthur's.

"My lady?"

Guinevere turned to look down at Ailis, smiling prettily. The queen was no longer the young woman she had been when she first came to Camelot, but her beauty remained intact, and her wits likewise.

And yet those eyes, normally sharp with intelligence, looked dulled now, as though the queen were having trouble focusing.

"My lady, is all well?"

"Indeed. It is simply . . . I find myself wearying of all this." The queen gestured at the entire hall. "But it pleases Arthur to send them off with such frolic."

"Yes, my lady." Ailis bowed and backed away. But her frown deepened as she noted others at the high table looking as—there was no other word for it—sleepy.

Something wasn't right. But the queen's taster, a bright-eyed lad, one of Guinevere's cousins from her home of Cameliard, was still alert and healthy, so it was not anything in the food. Indeed, Ailis had eaten and drunk much the same, sneaking bits from half full plates as they were carried out, and she felt fine.

It may all be my imagination, Ailis thought. *I'd look a proper fool if I said anything.* Nodding in agreement with herself, she tucked the dirty linens into the fold of her skirt and headed for the laundry, where she could leave them and then return. Some fresh air and all would be well.

*   *   *

The stuffed peacock had been the success Cook promised; even Gerard had to admit that. Four pages had staggered into the hall under its weight, the tail feathers spread in an astonishing display, and the flesh golden brown and filled to bursting with spiced meats. The squire had managed to be near Sir Rheynold when it was brought in, the better to see his master's reaction when Arthur saluted him for his contribution.

The pleasure the knight took in his triumph, however, was soon overtaken by a look of puzzlement on his face.

"Sir?" Gerard stepped forward, one hand raised

in a conscious gesture of aid.

"Hmmm?" Sir Rheynold looked up at him, his eyes creased with exhaustion. "Can't drink as much as I used to, I suppose," the knight murmured, slightly confused. "Don't remember it getting so late . . ."

Gerard lunged to catch his master as he slid side-wise on his bench. Pushing him back onto his seat and propping him against the wooden table, Gerard glanced around, panicked that someone might have seen the old man's embarrassment.

But instead, as the bells in the courtyard church struck the midnight hour, every adult in the hall—from the broad-shouldered form of the king himself down to the wiry-limbed jugglers performing before him—all slowed their movements, stilled, and fell limply where they stood.

The pages running the endless chores also slowed and then stopped, looking about them as they tried to understand what was happening. Some, smaller and younger than the others, burst into tears of confusion.

"Gerard?" Ailis's voice, small and scared, came from behind him. "What's happening? Why are they all . . . are they all . . . dead?"

TWO

Two of the younger pages began to bawl, sitting on the rush-strewn floor with tears rolling down their chubby faces. Other pages ran from table to table, some of them intent on finding an adult who was still awake, others grabbing whatever food or drink looked good off the table. Several of the tumblers' children were tugging at their elders who had fallen over their balls and hoops, while somewhere in the hall one of the younger children started to wail, her voice high pitched and keening. Gerard felt a pain start behind his eyes from the noise. He scanned the room, hoping desperately for someone—even Cook!—to come forward and explain what was happening. But all the adults he could see were slumped and motionless.

"They're sleeping." Finan, a squire in Sir

Danforth's service, gave one of the visiting knights' arms a rough shake. When there was no response, he stood up and faced Gerard. "The adults are all asleep."

"All of them? How?" Mak asked.

"How should I know?" Finan was freckled and red-haired, and so skinny that even on a feast day he looked as though he were about to die of starvation. But he was a good squire—one of the best with a lance, even if he was hesitant to take charge in any situation. "It's only us who are still awake."

Ailis spoke again, her voice steady despite the fear that was sweeping the room. "Do you think it's happened to everyone . . . throughout the castle?"

Gerard turned to Ailis; he'd been about to ask the question she had just voiced. Their earlier disagreement was forgotten as they stared at each other, the situation at hand almost too horrifying to accept. Adults couldn't just fall asleep all of a sudden. Not all of them. That didn't happen!

"Wait here," he said to her. Then he looked at Finan, including him in the order. "Try to keep the little ones calm. I'll be right back."

Outside the Great Hall, the corridors were empty and oddly silent. Camelot was like a beehive, as Sir

Rheynold always complained. The castle hummed with activity every hour of every day. But now, for the first time Gerard could remember, the beehive was still.

"Is anyone there?" Gerard called down the hallway, walking forward with his shoulders hunched as though expecting to be attacked at any moment. Or perhaps to fall asleep as suddenly as the knights and revelers had. A faint noise answered him. He hurried his steps and threw open a wooden door to reveal a very young page, clutching one of Arthur's hounds and sobbing his heart out. The dog looked up at Gerard with large, mournful brown eyes, as though to say "What could I do? The little one grabbed me and won't let go."

The boy was safe enough with the hound, and Gerard had other rooms to explore.

He went first toward the kitchen. It was the busiest place on a normal day, thrice so on a feast day. If anyone with authority were still awake, they would be there.

What greeted him, however, was not encouraging. Where earlier in the day the kitchen had moved with purpose and order, now it limped, blindly feeling its way. The youngest children were still turning the spit on which a boar roasted over the flames.

Three small figures—boys or girls, you couldn't tell under the flour that dusted them—were at the huge wooden table in the middle of the room, trying desperately to gather the pastry scraps to roll into something resembling a pie crust. Another child—no more than seven or eight—fed wood into a small fire by the far wall, while a taller one stirred a great black pot that simmered with the smell of warmed cider and made Gerard's stomach rumble. Despite everything that had happened, his body was still concerned about being fed.

Cook's massive form had clearly fallen too close to one of the cookfires and been dragged away; Gerard saw soot and a few singe marks on the man's clothing. He lay on his back on the floor, the older assistants likewise scattered in sleeping disarray around him.

"What's happening?" one of the children called as he saw Gerard in the doorway, not pausing in his work as he spoke.

Gerard could only shake his head. Only ten remained awake in the kitchen, of the thirty or more bodies he could count, and the oldest of them looked perhaps all of eleven years old.

Thinking quickly, Gerard realized that he was

41

likely the oldest person still awake in the entire castle! It was a sobering thought. He put it aside for the moment in order to deal with more immediate problems.

"Come with me," he ordered the children. "No, wait, stay here." They were doing the right thing. If they couldn't get the adults to wake up, they would still need to eat. "Move the sleepers out of the way, and make sure the food doesn't burn. Don't worry about making anything more for the feast; nothing fancy, just basic foods. Can you do that?" He directed his questions to the oldest, most steady-looking of the bunch, a boy with huge brown eyes and a smudge of something dark across his face.

"Yes," the boy responded promptly, clearly relieved to be given specific instructions. As Gerard turned to leave, he heard the kitchen boy calling out instructions to the others in a sweet, piping voice.

Somehow Gerard didn't think anything else was going to be that easy. The sound of children's raised voices crying and shouting as he came closer to the Great Hall confirmed his fears. He bypassed the feast, instead heading to the huge outer doors and into the courtyard. Perhaps whatever was happening was restricted to the building itself.

But outside, under the clear black sky, the situation was much the same. The guards posted to the castle's perimeter had slumped against the crenellations. Their dogs, cousins to the hound inside, sniffed anxiously at their masters' hands.

Gerard found himself retracing his steps of that afternoon, back to the stables. But inside, he found horses unattended and the stable workers asleep in the straw. Gerard looked for the stable boy he had fought with—Newt—but didn't see him among the sleepers. He paused to move some of the men who had fallen dangerously close to their charges' hooves, and made sure all the horses were secured, before going back into the Great Hall.

* * *

Inside the banquet hall, the chaos had worsened. Almost all the pages were crying now, and more than half the young servants had clearly given up, taking food off the tables and sitting in corners to eat. Gerard's stomach rumbled again loudly, a reminder that he hadn't had much to eat, either.

"Hey!" he yelled, trying to project his voice into the corners of the room.

The noise went on, the children ignoring his shout as though it had never been voiced.

43

"Listen to me!" he yelled again, drawing his voice up from the pit of his chest, the way Sir Bors said to do on a battlefield.

Ailis, across the hall with half a dozen of the youngest children gathered around her, didn't even look up.

"You haven't the voice for it."

Gerard turned and glared at the speaker—Newt the stable boy. What was he doing here? He was still wearing the same stained clothing from their fight, his hair had hay in it, and his eye, Gerard was glad to see, was black and blue and swollen, but his expression was distracted as he scanned the hall. "Nobody's going to listen to a squire with a squeaky voice."

The fact that Gerard's voice hadn't yet settled into a grown man's tones had been a matter of much teasing, some not so gentle, in recent months. Try as he might not to care, the taunt hurt.

It was true. He didn't sound commanding enough. Not like a knight at all.

"When in doubt," Sir Rheynold always lectured, "stand as tall as you can and do what you must."

"What does a stable boy know about leading anyone except horses?" he asked and strode across the hall to the high table where his king and court still sat, slumped and sleeping. Setting his jaw hard against the thought of what might happen if they should suddenly wake up, Gerard vaulted himself onto the wooden table and stood in the middle of the remains of the feast. He took a deep breath, let it out, and took in another. Then—

"Be QUIET!" he roared, pulling every memory of every time Sir Bors had ever yelled at the squires, and pitching his voice deep, to carry better.

It worked. Not every child was silenced, but enough of them. And they all looked up at Gerard.

"Crying and panicking won't wake them up," Gerard declared as sternly as he could manage. "Sitting around stuffing our faces"—the young players and servants who had been doing exactly that looked down at their plates, then back at him, some in shame—"won't wake them up. And neither of those things will protect us if whoever did this comes after us next."

"Oh, that was wise," Newt said, coming to stand beside the table. "Scare the little ones some more, why don't you?"

"They should be scared," Ailis said. She still held one of the pages by the hand, his tear-stained face now looking up at her trustingly. "We all should be.

How long do you think Camelot will stand if our enemies hear of what's happened?"

"What exactly *has* happened?" Newt asked, not unreasonably. He shoved his unruly black hair out of his eyes and stared around at the others, challenging them. "Every adult's fallen asleep. That's not exactly a dire situation."

"It might have been meant to kill them, and Merlin's protection spells turned it away," Ailis suggested.

"Or the spell wasn't meant to kill them," Gerard said. "Just leave them vulnerable. A captive is worth more than a corpse."

One of the tumblers, a scrawny, black-eyed boy, overheard them. "It's sorcery," he said loud enough for everyone nearby to hear.

"Of course it is," Gerard said scornfully, astonished that even a servant could be so foolish as to not realize that by now. "What else could it be?"

The tumbler looked for support among his fellows, but finding none, he backed away leaving only the three of them, Gerard, Newt, and Ailis, standing there.

"I know you," she said to Newt. "You're the hound boy."

"I was," he said. "Now I'm the horse boy."

Gerard ignored them and looked over the room, doing a quick mental count. Of the castle regulars who could be trusted to be useful, there were seven other squires still awake: Mak, Dewain, Finan, Robert, Tynan, Thomas, and Patrick. There were eleven servants, including Ailis. And Newt, he supposed. Another twenty pages, maybe, and ten of the players' children. Gerard had no idea how many children there were in Camelot itself. Ailis might know. She was a girl; they noticed things like that.

The squires came forward at Gerard's hand signal, gathering around him as he got down from the table.

"We need to organize," Patrick said, his eyes darting back and forth, his pale skin slick with sweat. "Burn a signal fire, ask for help."

"From who?" Finan asked, practical in the face of Patrick's obvious terror. "Like the mouse saying to the cat, 'Oh come help me, my tail's stuck!'"

"You think sitting around waiting is any better?" Patrick was the largest of the squires, muscled from years of weapons practice, and Gerard was more than a little afraid of him. Not that the other boy would ever hurt anyone . . . but sometimes he just didn't know when too much was too much, even in mock fighting.

Mak moved to get between the two of them, his own voice raised, and two of the servants who were still hanging back watching started to whisper to each other.

"Enough!" His voice cracked on the last syllable, but Gerard kept talking. "We can't stand around here saying what if and maybe. Mak, we need to have someone on the wall, keeping watch. You know the pages." Mak's younger brother was among them. "Find some of the older ones who can be trusted and set them there with the order to sound an alarm if they see anything—anything at all."

Mak nodded, reaching out to snag a black-haired page who had been lurking behind him. "Go find my brother. Tell him to meet me at the front gate with five of his best." The page, clearly terrified but used to being given run-and-fetch orders, nodded once and darted away.

"Who put you in charge?" the stable boy asked, standing among the squires as though he had the right to that company.

Gerard looked the other boy up and down and shrugged. It was a move he had seen the king use several times when humoring someone who had no right to ask questions but would be answered anyway. "I am the oldest squire awake. I have the most training. And"—he never played this trump, not out loud, but to this insolent servant he would—"I am the nephew of King Arthur himself, and so the closest to royal blood in Camelot."

He had no real claim to royal blood. Arthur was Sir Kay's foster brother; they had been raised together, but there were no blood ties between them. Sir Kay was Gerard's mother's brother, so he was really related to Kay, but not to Arthur. But hadn't Arthur welcomed him as family when he came to court? Didn't he call him nephew? It should count. It had to count.

The stable boy looked at him grudgingly, then nodded. Gerard's opinion of him went up . . . slightly. Sir Rheynold said that a man who could take correction well and without argument was a man worth having by your side. Even if he was a servant.

"So what are the rest of us to do?" Finan asked.

Gerard didn't know. Taking care of the watch had been the first thing he thought of, the first thing his training led him to cover, but after that . . . his mind went blank.

"We need to get these youngsters settled down," Newt said. "And . . . it's a little disrespectful, don't you think, to have your *uncle* slumped down in his food?" That was directed at Gerard, who blushed a little in anger that he hadn't thought of that as well.

"Combine the two," Robert said. "I'll make it into a game for them." He nodded once to Gerard, gave a shorter acknowledgment to Newt, and turned to gather up some of the more alert-looking children. Within minutes, they were swarming all over the hall, lifting adult heads off the tables, wiping faces, cleaning up spills, and setting the sleepers upright in their chairs like so many life-sized dolls.

Patrick scowled at the activity. "We need help," he said again.

"We need Merlin," Ailis said, then stared back at the boys when they swung on her as though the cat had spoken. "What? It's an enchantment, isn't it? And he's an enchanter, isn't he? Moreover, he's *the king's* enchanter. So who else would be able to help?"

"Assuming he hasn't done it himself," Robert muttered. "He always was a weird one."

Gerard, remembering his odd encounter with the wizard months earlier, had to agree. But still, Arthur trusted the enchanter. He had always trusted him. Impossible to believe Merlin would turn on that trust now.

"So where is Merlin the enchanter?" Newt asked. "If he's asleep, he's not much use to us or his king."

"He's gone," Gerard said flatly. "He stormed out of the castle a couple of months back." He still remembered the sound of the front gate slamming shut not by human hands, but by a magical wind that swirled in Merlin's wake.

Robert nodded his head, remembering. "Huge row with the king. Hasn't been seen since. He does that every now and then—picks a fight, disappears. I think he does it because he's bored."

"A bored enchanter is a dangerous thing," Dewain said, as though he knew the danger firsthand.

"He wasn't bored," Ailis disagreed.

"Right. And you know that—how? Does Merlin confide in you?" Dewain was scornful, taking his uncertainty out on her.

"I was there," she said defiantly, her expression daring them to challenge her further. "In the room, when the argument began." She paused, obviously trying to remember exactly what happened. "Arthur said something about the Quest, although he didn't call it that, then. He called it . . . a mission? And Merlin said there were other things they should be worried about, like the unhappiness someone was stirring up among the border lords, and . . . and

problems inside the castle, too. And Arthur agreed
and wanted Merlin to do something about it, and
Merlin said he couldn't—that he was going to be
somewhere else then, and no, he couldn't tell Arthur
where because he didn't know yet, and then it got
sort of confusing."

There were nods of acceptance around the group.
Any discussion with Merlin was bound to become
confusing, living backward in time the way he did.
Not that any of them really understood what it meant,
but it *sounded* confusing. And none of the adults
seemed to understand it either, except the king.

"What all that means is that we have no idea
where the only person who could help us is," Robert
said glumly.

"We know he didn't approve of the Quest,"
Tynan pointed out. "Isn't this the sort of thing an
enchanter might do to *stop* the Quest?"

"If he wanted to stop the Quest, he could have
done it without leaving," Mak said, giving Tynan a
look of contempt. "It would have been easier that
way. I don't trust Merlin; I don't trust any magic-
user. But he lives to serve Arthur, same as we all do.
And he was the one who sent out the message about
the Quest in the first place, so knights outside of

Camelot would know about it. Would someone who wanted to stop the Quest do that?"

"We'll find him." Gerard spoke before he realized it, then said more slowly, "I'll find him." It's what a knight would do, and he was the closest thing they had to a knight now. The others should stay behind, safe inside Camelot's walls, with Camelot's reputation to protect them—at least for a little while.

"And how do you plan to do that?" Newt asked, his expression skeptical but his voice neutral.

"Take me with you," Ailis said.

Everyone looked at Ailis, and she blushed red all the way up to her forehead. "I know Merlin. I mean, I've talked to him."

"So have I," Gerard retorted. Only once, true, but . . . "He knows who I am." Also true, if still more than a little frightening. "He said . . . he said that I had impressed him. *Would* impress him. So maybe he meant that I would find him when he was needed."

"That's thin." Tynan waved a hand in dismissal of the idea.

"It's more than anyone else has."

"If he's such a great enchanter, why doesn't he know his king's been put under a spell?" Newt spoke again, his chin jutting out stubbornly.

"I don't know! I don't know how he thinks. I don't *want* to know how he thinks! If you have a better idea, then tell me." Gerard didn't quite fling his arms up into the air in complete frustration, but it was close.

Robert couldn't refrain from giving his opinion. "I hate magic. Give me a good sword and a strong horse. They make sense. This doesn't."

"It's an attack," Finan said. "There are only two things you can do in the face of an attack. Defend or retreat."

"Or find allies," Patrick insisted.

"You find Merlin. We'll defend," Finan said.

The other squires said, "Aye" in agreement, their faces now showing excitement and the desire to prove themselves, in place of the former fear and uncertainty.

"Take me with you," Ailis said again, stamping her foot on the floor, impatient at being ignored while the boys talked.

"Ailis, you're—" She fixed Gerard with a stare that made him rethink what he was going to say. "You're needed here," he went on. "You've been here forever, you know how everything runs. Take care of everyone. Run the castle. When the chatelaine wakes

up, she'll be so impressed she'll move you straight-
away into . . . doing whatever it is you want to do."

"Urrrgghh." The servant girl ground her teeth in
frustration. "You can't go alone."

"Then take me." Newt had been silent, standing
on the outskirts of the discussion, but now he stepped
forward, his gaze intent on Gerard's face. "I know
the roads. I know how to forage and how to scout.
The beasts in the stable can be fed by any whelp, so
long as they're able to hold a bucket. And I'd do no
good in the running of things in here." He waved an
arm, indicating the chaos inside and the walls that
needed to be defended outside.

Gerard stared at the stable boy, trying to judge
the offer. It seemed sincere. He didn't like him, but
Ailis was right: Two of them would be safer on the
roads than one. Be fair, he reminded himself. You
don't have to like someone to work with them.

"I'm in command." It wasn't a question.

Newt shrugged, neither agreeing nor arguing.
Gerard eyed him suspiciously, then declared, "All
right. We leave at first light."

The boys moved off in a group, discussing strate-
gies for either finding Merlin or defending the castle.
Ailis, left behind, bit the inside of her cheek to keep

the tears from spilling over. She wasn't sure if she was more scared or angry. She knew she could help. She *knew* it.

Foolish child. Come to me.

Ailis started, not sure if she had really heard the voice in her head or imagined it. She looked around the banquet room. The squires and pages and other children had left. She was the only one awake in the Great Hall.

At first there was only the unnatural silence of the sleeping court. Then, every bit as strange, she heard the voice again.

Child, hurry.

She was certain she hadn't imagined that. "Merlin?" she asked uneasily.

But there was no answer. The voice was gone.

THREE

Birds chirped and tweeted outside the stable, heralding the first light of dawn. Newt lay on his straw pallet in the back of the stable, surrounded by sleeping bodies—both human and canine. It was all perfectly normal . . . except for the fact that not one of his fellow servants was snoring. The grooms and the stable master had all fallen under the spell.

Newt couldn't remember a morning of his life when he hadn't woken to the sound of snores.

"Something to be said for spells," he told himself as he rolled out from under a coarse blanket, shoved one of the hounds off his pallet, and ran a hand through his hair. No use to even try and tame it—he was born with hair going all different directions, and he would die that way.

Moving past the sleeping bodies, he gave a passing

caress to the inquisitive equine noses thrust over stall doors, and emerged into the dawn, blinking sleepily. A bucket of cool water pulled from the well got him reasonably clean and awake, as much as he could be on only a handful of hours of sleep. His face still hurt, but the bruises from his tussle with the squire seemed to be fading already.

Had that fight really only been yesterday? It seemed years ago. Magic did that. It made time strange. Time and people. He had hoped never to be entangled in anything even smelling like magic ever again, and here he was, in the thick of it.

No, in the thick of it would mean I'd be sleeping, he thought, his sense of humor reasserting itself as he woke up a little more.

Newt went back into the stables, packed his few belongings into a leather saddlebag, and placed it carefully over a stall door.

"Stop that," he said to the bay mare who tried to nibble on the straps of the pack. "You'll be fed soon enough." He hoped. Bold words, to volunteer himself for this fool's errand, but he doubted the ability of even the best squire to keep these beauties in line and cared for. What was he thinking, to leave them? His life was here; his purpose was here, with these animals.

Newt smiled wryly. He was thinking that for all his brave posturing and loud words, the king's nephew would be lost on the road by himself. Newt would wager money he didn't have that the boy had never been on his own for a night, much less a whole journey to who knew where. If this trek to find the enchanter was to succeed, Newt would be needed.

Tugging his boots on and knocking the worst of the horse dung from them, Newt made one last futile attempt at making his water-slicked hair behave. He set his still-aching jaw and walked the unfamiliar distance from the stable to the great wooden doors of the castle.

Stable boys, like servants, didn't use the main entrance. He hadn't been thinking clearly the night before when he'd run through these gates to see if what had struck the stable could be explained by someone in power. Now, though, the very act of walking on the polished stone floors made his heart shake in fear, half expecting someone to grab him by the ear and toss him back into the straw where he belonged.

But no one did.

The only souls he saw in the hallways were two pages, red-eyed and rumpled. Newt tapped one on the shoulder, feeling guilty when the boy jumped as though he'd been bit on the rump.

"Where's the squire Gerard?"

The smaller and blonder of the pages pointed down the hallway. "In the Room."

"The what?" The entire castle was made of nothing but rooms!

"The Room. The Council Room," the boy said in a tone that clearly indicated his opinion of anyone who needed it spelled out for them.

"Where is it?"

Directions pried out of the boy, Newt patted him on the head out of sheer maliciousness, and went in search of his road companion.

The great doors were closed, but the smaller door set into them was open. Newt walked in, hearing his boots echo in a way they hadn't anywhere else. The squire—Gerard, Newt reminded himself—was standing by the table, one hand resting on the polished surface.

"It's just a table," Newt said. He had been expecting something . . . more.

The squire didn't seem to hear him, staring down into the polished wooden surface as though it were a scrying mirror.

"It's not just a table," Gerard said finally. His voice was raw and raspy from lack of sleep, and it made Newt's throat hurt just to hear it. "It's a symbol. Symbols are important. Sometimes they're all we have."

"Yeah. Right." Newt wanted to be out of this room. It weighed on him, a pressure on the back of his head like a disapproving stare. He knew he didn't belong here.

The squire turned to look at him then. His blue eyes were as red-rimmed as the young pages' had been. Was Newt the only one to have gotten any sleep at all?

"You're ready to go?" Gerard asked.

The night before, Newt had picked out the horses they would take: two sturdy beasts from Camelot's own stable; quality riding horses, a gelding for him and an older bay stallion that he knew the squires had been training on, neither of them too showy nor overly muscled from combat. He had also arranged for the kitchen brats to provision them as best they could from what was available. Dried meats and bread, probably. "If you know where we're going."

"I've an idea," was all the squire said. And with that, Newt had to be satisfied.

* * *

The sun was just beginning to lift over the hills behind Camelot when they finally led their horses and a heavily laden mule out of the great gate.

"You know where we're going?" Newt asked for the tenth time. And for the tenth time Gerard answered, "I've an idea."

"I hate you," Newt told him matter-of-factly.

To the stable boy's surprise, the squire laughed a clear, shining note. "More so now than when I bested you in fight?"

"You did no such thing," Newt retorted, swinging into the saddle and gathering up the reins. His companion did the same, moving with ease despite the boiled leather armor that buckled over his chest and lower legs.

"I would have, if Lancelot hadn't stopped us."

"You're dreaming," Newt said and kicked his gelding into an easy trot, forcing the squire to keep up with him, not the other way around as would have been expected.

"You're an ignorant servant who smells of horse."

If the squire thought that was going to insult him, he had a lot to learn. Horse was what he tended, horse was what he would smell like. It was an honest smell.

They continued in that manner all day, trading mild insults to ward off the fear that lingered just below the surface, until the sun began to set into the western hills. Before the light faded, they found a small stream, hobbled the horses and mule beside it to graze in the soft grasses, then took the pack off the mule.

Out of the pack—and Gerard suspected Ailis's hand in it more than the stable boy's vague directions to the servant children—the squire took two blankets and set them down on the ground where there seemed to be the fewest stones. Meanwhile the stable boy gathered twigs and branches from a nearby copse of trees to build a fire with.

It wasn't the way knights would have done it. Knights would have come with more than just one pack animal, and they would have had the proper equipment to raise a simple tent, or perhaps even a pavilion with their banner flying from the top post. They wouldn't have made do with rough blankets on the ground and a small fire to ward off the darkness and heat the bread and cheese they had brought to supplement the game they were too weary to hunt.

No, a knight would have handled things much better. But all the knights lay asleep in Camelot's Great Hall.

"I'm sorry, Sir Rheynold," Gerard said to his absent and sleeping master. "I know you say that a good knight always has a plan. I don't have a plan. I have a hunch. A thought. A maybe. But a maybe is nothing to ride out on."

His words were directed up to the stars, but the sound barely carried past his lips. Across the fire, Newt lay on his side, one arm flung over his face, his breathing heavy and nasal in sleep. It might have been any other night of his life, the way he had dropped off into slumber.

Gerard envied him, for the moment he himself lay down, it seemed every rock in the vicinity had crawled to rest under him, digging into his flesh no matter how he turned or twisted. And likewise, their journey dug into his mind.

"I so wanted to join the Quest. I wanted to be part of the Grail's finding, make my reputation, earn my spurs so that everyone would know my name. And now I—"

Something in the bushes beyond the fire sneezed.

Newt went from sound asleep to wide awake in

the time it took Gerard to come to his feet and grab his scabbard from its resting place. The sword, a sturdy but unlovely length of metal, was gifted to him when he turned ten and was judged ready for a man's weapon. It rested heavy in his hands.

Newt, his dagger likely to be useless in this situation, scooted on his hands and knees toward the bushes that had just sneezed, ready to lunge. Gerard watched until Newt was within tackling distance of whatever it was.

"Show yourself!" Gerard called, willing his voice not to crack. Thankfully, this once, it heeded him.

The bushes remained still and silent.

Gerard looked at Newt, who stayed focused on the area the sneeze had come from. His posture was terrible; any half-trained page could take him out. But, remembering their fight, Gerard allowed that the other boy might be useful in an unarmed scuffle if it came to that. Besides, Newt was all he had to work with.

"Show yourself!" Gerard demanded again, and when there was no response, he made a sharp gesture with his free hand, indicating that Newt should move forward. Newt couldn't have seen it, but charged anyway, lunging into the shrubbery headfirst.

"Ow!"

"What is it? What happened?" Gerard pulled his sword fully out of the scabbard and moved forward, keeping half his attention on the surrounding area, aware that an ambush could come from any direction, at any time.

Newt reemerged from the bushes, holding one hand to his face. His other hand came forward to show off—

"A rabbit?" Gerard didn't know if he should be relieved or angry.

Newt shrugged. "They scream when they die. Why not a sneeze?"

Gerard looked at the dun-colored beast twitching in Newt's grasp and started to laugh weakly as he resheathed his sword.

"I suppose at least we have breakfast for tomorrow."

Newt looked at the rabbit, then at Gerard. "I caught it. You kill it."

"You think I can't?" Gerard bristled at the suggestion. He hadn't had to do such a thing in years, but he was sure he would remember how. Pretty sure, anyway.

Newt shrugged, holding the rabbit out for the

squire to take. In the firelight the small beast seemed almost misshapen, demonic. Gerard stared at it, then looked up at Newt.

"Oh, for heaven's sake . . ." Newt started to say, then opened his hand and let the animal fall to the ground. It recovered the instant its paws touched dirt, and with two strong hops disappeared back into cover.

Gerard blinked at the expression on Newt's face: part anger, part embarrassment, and purely defiant.

"It wouldn't have kept well on the road, anyway," was all the other boy said. "I'm going back to sleep."

But sleep didn't come for either one of them. They started and turned at every sound in the night, until dawn found them both awake and ready to move on. A full day and then some had passed since their world turned upside down, and Gerard found himself wondering about the castle. Were they all still safe? Did anyone outside Camelot know?

"Get up with you," Newt muttered to the mule, tugging at one of its elongated ears. "We're not on a pleasure trip, you know." The mule made a rude noise at him, bit a tuft of his hair, and got a solid thwap on its rear in return.

"If you're done making love noises at your lady . . ." Gerard began, already saddled and mounted.

"At least I have one," Newt retorted. He kneed the mule gently in the gut to make sure it wasn't holding its breath against the packs and, satisfied, hooked the lead rope to his beast's saddle and mounted. The gelding sidestepped at the weight, then settled down once Newt picked up the reins. He might not be the rider the squire was, but he knew horses better. You took what satisfaction you could. And if it was petty and foolish, so what? It still felt good.

*   *   *

The sun was at their shoulders when Newt heard the noise. It wasn't much of anything—it might have been the stream that ran alongside the path they were riding on. Or a squirrel in the trees to their left. Or even a bird following them for some reason known only to birds.

But he didn't think so.

Digging his heels into the gelding's sides, Newt moved up to ride alongside Gerard. The look on the squire's face was carefully blank, but his eyes were moving back and forth and there was a drop of sweat on his forehead that couldn't be explained by the cool weather or the easy pace they were keeping.

"Wasn't a rabbit last night," Newt said quietly.

"I figured that one out already."

Nice to see nerves didn't make him any softer. Was it something they learned when they became squires? The pages always seemed decent enough, until they jumped up the next level and became too good to talk to servants. The knights were a different matter again. Some good, some not. All too full of themselves. Except Lancelot. Lance was different all over.

"Your horse is going lame," Gerard said.

Newt was startled out of his thoughts by the comment. "He is not! I've never had a horse. . . . You just don't want to talk about whatever was in our camp last night, do you?"

"He's limping. Get down and take a look. He probably has something in his shoe. You were too hasty in grooming him last night."

They had spent exactly the same amount of time grooming the night before. In fact, the squire had asked Newt's opinion on a gash on his horse's foreleg while he was checking for stones in . . . *oh.* That was the game, was it?

Newt pulled the gelding to the side of the narrow path and dismounted. He looped the reins over one arm as he bent down on the far side, his back to the creek, as though oblivious to anything except his horse.

He froze at a quiet crunching sound coming from somewhere in the stand of oak trees behind them.

There it was again, louder without the sound of hooves to mask it. They were definitely being followed! He glanced up at the squire, wondering if Gerard had heard it.

Gerard moved his beast forward a few steps, as though impatient to be on his way. "Fool of a horse-boy," he said, the sneer evident in his voice. "Catch up with me when you're done. And mind the mule doesn't go lame as well with your inept handling."

And with that he kicked his horse into a trot and moved down the path, around a bend, and out of sight.

Muttering under his breath, Newt pushed against his gelding until it lifted its front right leg enough so that any observer would see him check for the alleged stone lodged in the hoof.

"Easy, boy. Easy. Let me just see what's ailing you, hey?" He kept up the soothing patter, hoping that the beast would hear only the familiar words, and not the nerves underlying them. He strained his ears for the sound of their unknown companion, or maybe the sound of Gerard doubling back to—

"Hai!" Gerard's shout was followed by a loud, high-pitched yelp of outrage. Newt dropped the horse's leg and the reins as well, and dashed to the other side of the animal in time to see two figures tumbling down the hill from the tree line. The gelding snorted nervously, and Newt reached back to catch at his mane, patting him soothingly while he watched the two scrabbling in a tangle of legs and arms.

Finally Gerard got the upper hand, reaching up to grab at his opponent's face, which was covered by a close-fitting hood.

The hood came away in his hand, revealing a long red braid attached to a familiar head.

"Ailis?" Gerard sounded like he had swallowed a frog.

The servant girl rolled away from the squire, his grasp weakened by shock. Sitting back on her heels, she glared at him.

"What—what are you doing here?" Newt asked in disbelief.

Gerard slapped at the cloth of his trousers, trying

to get the dirt out of them, and glared sourly back at the girl. "That's the obvious part. She was following us. The real question is, how fast can she go home?"

"I'm not going back. You need me."

"We do not." Gerard looked stubborn enough to be part mule.

"Yes you do! Neither of you knows the first thing about Merlin."

"And you do?" Disbelief colored the squire's voice.

"More than you!" Ailis clearly wanted to say more but bit it back.

Despite himself, Newt was curious. Most of the girls he knew were quiet mice, their faces down-turned, their attention focused on their tasks. But this girl glared back at the squire as if she were his equal. She had stood up to them back in the banquet hall. She was different. *Why?*

"Witless servant," Gerard muttered.

"Fool of a squire," she returned.

"Might as well let her stay," Newt said, already tired of watching the two of them spat like cats. He had a feeling he was going to regret this. "I suspect she'll only follow anyway. And I'm a lousy cook, besides."

*   *   *

"So. What's the plan? We do have a plan, don't we?" Ailis said.

Newt looked up from the roasted pigeon he was eating, his expression alertly curious. "I've been wondering that as well," he admitted. "Not that a mere servant like myself—ourselves"—he made a mocking gesture toward Ailis—"need to know such things, when a mighty knight-in-training has it all in order." Two days in Gerard's company, and Newt had already figured out how far he could push the squire without rousing the other boy's true anger. Mocking merely irritated him.

"Oh, stuff it," Gerard said rudely, biting into his own roasted squab. "This is good," he said to Ailis, who merely shrugged off the compliment. They had caught the birds that afternoon; she had only cooked them. She was seated by the fire, now wearing a drab brown wool skirt pulled from the leather bag she had carried with her. Her top was a simple tunic taken from one of the squires, creating an oddly mismatched appearance.

"Plan?" she prompted her companion. Newt could tease, if it amused him to do so. An advantage of knowing Gerard for so many years was that she could dispense with that when there were more important things to do. She would get to annoying him later, when he really deserved it.

"I have a map," Gerard admitted, slowly.

"A map?" Ailis looked delighted. "That's wonderful. A map of what?"

"Of . . ." Gerard looked deeply uncomfortable. "Of places."

"Most maps are of places," she agreed, folding her hands in her lap and patiently waiting for more information. It infuriated him, she knew. All the more so because he knew she wasn't going to give up. And from the look on Newt's face, neither was he.

"Arrrrgh." Gerard put his bird down on one of the slabs of bark they were using for platters and stared into the coals of the fire. They had covered only a short distance today, nowhere near where he wanted to be by this point. And meanwhile, the adults and his king slept. And the kingdom was at risk because of it.

"A map of places King Arthur used to go. Back before he was king, when he was Merlin's student and they used to go wandering."

"Before he married the queen," Ailis said, nodding. "I remember hearing stories." The king and queen had been married the year before she and

Gerard came to Camelot; years before Newt worked in the stables. "Where did you get such a map?"

"He stole it," Newt said suddenly. "Didn't you?"

Gerard snarled soundlessly. "It wasn't as though there was anyone awake I could ask, was there?"

"Where did you take it from?"

"Thekingsstudy." He said it fast, the words running into each other.

"What?" Ailis wasn't sure if she heard him correctly, or if the strain of trying to keep up with them on foot for a full day was making her hear things.

"The. King's. Study."

She hadn't been hearing things.

"You stole something from the king's private study?" Ailis wasn't sure if she was more horrified or mortified.

"Wonderful," Newt said in disgust. "Why not take something from Merlin's own bed while you're at it?"

"Because I'd look very bad as a rat," Gerard said, tearing the last flesh off his bird and tossing the bones into the coals. "And there wasn't anything there that was useful, far as I could tell. This looked like it might be." He reached back into his pack, which he was using as a backrest, and carefully drew out a wooden tube. Inside was a parchment. He unrolled it and placed it on the ground, weighting it down with a rock he pulled from the circle around the fire, careful to choose one that wasn't too warm.

Someone had drawn the outline of the isle in a clear, dark hand. The three could recognize the mark that indicated Camelot, and the one that showed Cameliard, the queen's home, but—

"What's that?" Newt asked.

"Cymry."

"Oh. And that?" He pointed to another mark.

The three of them gathered closer, craning their heads. "I don't know," Gerard admitted finally. There was writing in the margins of the map. But from the expressions on his companions' faces, Gerard assumed that neither of them could decipher the crabbed and faded writing, either.

"What're those symbols?" Newt asked, pointing to the strange sigil that appeared all over the map in a thin brown ink.

"It's Merlin's mark," Ailis said. She was careful not to touch it, and Newt moved his finger away hastily.

Gerard nodded, taking the parchment and carefully rolling it up again. "I think Arthur made this to keep track of where Merlin wandered. Where his favorite places were."

"So we'll look in those marked places first?" Ailis asked.

"It's somewhere to start," Gerard said with a shrug. "He's not been gone that long, so we'll head north, begin with the closest and work our way out as needed."

Neither of the others mentioned that an enchanter need not travel by normal means, and that Merlin might be anywhere by now. Their entire quest was a fool's errand anyway. Why make it worse by admitting it out loud?

FOUR

"Do you think they've woken yet?" Newt asked.

"No." Gerard didn't even bother to shake his head. He was staring at the road ahead of them with more concentration than the flat path deserved. He didn't have to ask who "they" were. The adults. Camelot.

"No." Ailis mulled over the word. "I don't think so, either." Not that anyone could have found them to tell them the news, if they had.

She was riding a horse now—an unnamed, rangy, torn-eared roan gelding with white-rimmed eyes. It looked uglier than a toad, but Newt had picked it out that morning from the others that the local farrier was willing to sell, having sorted through the herd with a practiced eye. Gerard hadn't wanted to spend the coins, since they only had what the squires had been able to pool together, but riding double was slowing them down too much, and the mule flat-out refused to carry any more weight in addition to their supplies.

They'd been away from Camelot heading northeast for two days now, following Gerard's map to the nearest of the sigil-marked locations. The narrow track had widened into a true road, the dirt packed down by years of wagon traffic moving from town to town. The trees to their left were balanced by the meadows on their right, filled with quail and rabbits that Gerard proved very good at catching for their evening meals.

Though she was glad they weren't going hungry, Ailis was getting sick of meat for every meal. And she hadn't been able to wash properly since she left Camelot; her scalp itched under her braid, tucked up again under her hood, and she was pretty sure she smelled like dirty horse and dried sweat. Still, if their mission hadn't been so urgent, she might have been enjoying herself. But even if she hadn't shared the boys' fears about an unknown enemy lurking somewhere, waiting for word to attack the now-defenseless castle, the thought of her queen slumped over her meal was one she would never be able to wipe from her mind's eye—the indignity of it so at odds with her lady's bearing and desires. And so the fresh air, the new sights, and the freedom to wear a page's cast-off shirt and leggings under her skirt for modesty so she could sit astride like a boy was only half as sweet as it might have been.

"Town ahead," Gerard called back. He was riding a few paces in front, his horse more restless than their geldings.

"Finally." If they had gone west upon leaving Camelot, they would have encountered numerous towns built in the shadow of Camelot's walls. East and south were the ocean and the rocky cliffs that Merlin—according to the map—seemed to avoid. North was where the sigils were; where the land was less settled. There lay swathes of woodlands and meadows undisturbed in the years since Arthur took the throne and established the Pax Britannica, the peace of Britain. It was as though nobody wanted to live where so many had died in battle the year after Uther, Arthur's father, had fallen.

A shiver went through Ailis. Her parents had died in such a battle, although she had no memory of it herself.

"Blood fed those trees," Newt said, as though he had been reading her mind. Ailis forced her gaze away from the towering oaks and onto Gerard noting how he sat so straight in the saddle, even as he leaned forward to stroke his horse's neck.

"Are you superstitious?" she asked lightly, truly looking at Newt for the first time. The interesting roughness of his features, fading bruises and all, was a marked contrast from Gerard's narrow face and paler coloring, although Gerard was showing a few bruises himself. She wondered if there was a connection. Maybe that was why the two boys seemed so uneasy around each other. "Do you believe Ankou will come to collect you if you walk over the resting places of the dead?"

"Who?" He looked at her blankly.

"Ankou. The gatherer of the dead. Don't you listen to any of the old stories?"

"Not much place for stories in the stable," Newt said.

Since Ailis knew full well that the tales that didn't come from the kitchens came from the stables, she gave that claim the look of scorn it deserved, making Newt snort with laughter. His expression lightened and made him seem quite . . . presentable.

"What are you laughing at?" Gerard asked, falling back to rejoin them.

"The stable boy is being impossible," Ailis said primly, but her eyes were alight with mischief.

"He excels at that," Gerard said, shooting Newt a sideways glare. It wasn't quite a warning, it wasn't quite jealousy, but it clearly said "hands off." Ailis might be a servant, but she was a member of the queen's household and Gerard's friend, besides. Too good for a stable boy to flirt with.

"We need to talk about how we're going to approach this," Gerard said, intentionally moving his bay between Ailis's and Newt's horses.

"Approach what?" Newt asked.

"The townspeople. Or did you plan on riding in and asking, 'Excuse me, have you seen an errant enchanter? We require him most urgently back at Camelot'?"

Newt shrugged. "If it would get us the answers we need, yes."

"It wouldn't. They'd be more likely to hold us as horse thieves."

"Even a noble squire?" Newt was mocking, but Gerard refused to rise to the bait.

"Noble is as noble appears," Ailis said, gently leaning forward to pat her gelding's neck as it jerked at the reins.

Gerard scowled at that. He knew he didn't appear at all noble right now, in his worn leathers and second-best surcoat. By the holy cross, he would mistake himself for a horse thief if he didn't know better!

"You're well-born. You can speak the part, certainly. Newt is your servant. You were sent to . . . ah . . ." Ailis lost the story as she tried to determine what her role in all this might be.

"You're my sister," Newt said suddenly. "We're going to visit our father. Our master's son, for a lark, decided to join us. Against his father's wishes. We're looking for another old servant, who has since left the household. We have a message to bear him, from our master, which was why we were given leave to go. So it's vital we pass it along, else we risk our master's anger when we return without a response."

He stopped, suddenly realizing that the other two were staring at him as their horses plodded along down the road.

"What?" he asked defensively.

"You were wasted with beasts," Gerard said with an edge to his voice. "You should have been a troubadour."

"Now, that was unkind," Newt said, rubbing his chest over his heart as though mortally wounded.

The squire merely turned his attention back to the space between his horse's ears.

"It is sound," Ailis said, running it over in her thoughts. "His plan, I mean. Certainly better than anything I might come up with . . . and we haven't much time."

Since the sturdy brown walls of the unnamed town were coming into view, the boys had to agree.

"Let me do the talking, then," Ailis said quickly, sensing that Gerard was still unhappy with the plan—any plan—that Newt might come up with.

Unlike Camelot, this town had no guards outside its walls. The three companions rode through an untended gate, then past a low, long building that smelled of sheep, and a stone church without seeing a living soul. Several cottages, close together and bounded by a low stone wall and carefully tended hedges, looked more promising, but whoever lived in them stayed within.

"Over there." Gerard pointed toward one of the small cottages, and they moved their horses in the direction of a lone figure in its yard.

"Pardon, my lady," Ailis began.

The woman looked up from the shirts she was laying over flowering bushes to dry, and blinked at the odd trio in front of her.

"Pardon, but we're seeking a man—" Ailis faltered here. She was so accustomed to thinking of Merlin as an old man—he had, after all, helped to raise Arthur!—that she pictured him as one. They all did, else Newt would never have thought to cast him as an old servant, long retired. But describing him physically made her realize that he wasn't actually that old at all. In fact, since he was living backward, it was possible that he was actually getting younger.

Magic, she thought. *He doesn't just use magic, he* is *magic.* It was a new idea, an interesting idea, and one she didn't have time to follow right now.

"We're in search of a man—a former servant of my master, who chose to go out on his own. Our master tasked us to find him. We were told he might have taken shelter within your village. He is tall and slender. A hawk's beak of a nose, and dark hair shot with silver . . ."

Ailis let her voice trail off as the woman merely stared at her. They had no idea what name Merlin might be using, if indeed he used any name at all. Who knew what an enchanter might do? He might not even be in his own form—he might be traveling the countryside as an animal, as a bird; as the rabbit they had for dinner the night before! Ailis fought down nausea at the thought.

"Might you have seen such a man?" she finished.

The woman looked at each of them in turn, then shook her head. "Sparrows cry. The fox does not dine, but feathers fly."

The three of them stared at her and she looked back placidly, her wide-set brown eyes as calm as a faithful hound's.

"Right. Our thanks, madam," Gerard said finally, making a vaguely courtly bow from horseback, and reining his horse aside and back into the road. The other two followed, Newt more reluctantly than Ailis.

"Strange," Newt said.

"Mad," Gerard said flatly.

"She didn't seem to be mad," Ailis argued.

"Do you think they all froth at the mouth and roll in the dust?" Gerard shook his head. "Mad. Take my word for it."

"I've seen madwomen before," Newt disagreed. "She didn't strike me as such. There was awareness in her eyes, not madness."

"Her words were madness."

With that, Newt couldn't argue. Who but a madwoman spoke in such strange terms?

By the time the sun was shading into the hills, however, the three of them not only believed that every soul in the town was mad, they grew less certain about their own sanity. Every single person they had spoken to responded in the same nonsense patter as the first woman.

"If not mad, then cursed. The work of a sorcerer," Gerard decided.

"To speak gibberish? A strange curse." But Ailis could not explain what they had heard any other way.

They had finally collapsed, weary beyond words, by the well in the center of town. They had spent the day questioning one incomprehensible villager after another until all three felt as though their eyes were crossing from the effort of remaining polite. They had left the horses hobbled outside a small stable, paying the old man who ran it to keep an eye on their belongings, and wandered the town on foot, hoping that speaking eye-to-eye would give them better results. But no luck.

"Do you think they annoyed Merlin?" Newt wondered.

"Is there anyone who hasn't annoyed Merlin at one point or another? But most of Camelot still speaks plainly." Newt and Ailis both turned to look at Gerard in disbelief. He noted their stares and shrugged. "Court matters aside. All right, fine. At least they don't speak nonsense rhymes."

"Save when they attempt poetry," Ailis said and broke into exhausted giggles. "Have you *heard* some of it?"

"Too much," Gerard said in agreement. "But this isn't that sort of rhyming. It's . . ." But he couldn't put into words what was shifting in his mind.

"It's a mystery," Ailis said finally.

"It's magic. If Merlin comes here often, there has to be a reason. Maybe it's magic. There are places like that, right? Magical places? Well, magic changes people."

It wasn't the first time Newt had given his opinion on magic and it wasn't likely to be the last, so his companions ignored him.

The three of them sat on the edge of the well, so caught up in their own thoughts that they didn't notice the soft sound of feet coming toward them until the newcomer spoke.

"The owl, lonely flier."

Their gaze started low at the shoes, made of worn brown leather, then rose up past the layers of skirts and tunic, stopping finally at the wrinkled, wizened face of an old woman standing in front of them.

"Old mother?" Ailis asked. "You were saying?" The residents of this town might all be mad, but there was no reason to be unkind.

"The owl, lonely flier. Moonlight, water, what you desire."

She met their gazes, each individual in turn, then nodded firmly and shuffled off, her obligation seemingly fulfilled.

"More gibberish," Gerard said in disgust.

"No." Newt held up a hand. "I don't think so. It's not the words. It's what the words *say*. The people aren't mad; they just think differently." He turned to Gerard, his dark eyes alight with an intensity that took the others by surprise. "Give me the map."

"Wha—"

"The map!"

Gerard looked at Ailis, who nodded slowly. He withdrew the tube from the pack he had brought with him and handed it reluctantly to the other boy. Newt pulled the map out with clear impatience, almost tearing it in his hurry.

"Careful!" Ailis warned.

Newt unrolled the map and stared at it intently.

"There. And there."

"There what?"

"Water. The owl is Merlin—the lonely flier, the harbinger of death. That's what they call Merlin outside the castle when Arthur can't hear. Because whenever he showed up, battles followed. 'Moonlight, water, what you desire.' Water . . . there and there. Both are marked by a sigil." He pointed to the locations on the map—two lakes, one fairly close to the town they were in—careful not to accidentally let his fingers brush any of the magical sigils. He wasn't sure whether the inscriptions on the map had power, but anything connected with a sorcerer like Merlin called for caution.

"Where does moonlight come from?" Gerard asked.

"Where the moon would travel?" Newt guessed wildly. All three of them looked up into the sky, searching for that heavenly body.

"We'll have to wait until nightfall," Ailis said, disappointed.

"Do you think we could get something to eat that we didn't have to catch or cook?" Gerard wondered out loud, causing Ailis to pat him consolingly on the shoulder.

"Poor thing, worn to a wisp by burden of caring for yourself."

From Ailis it was teasing, and Gerard could take it with good grace. And when Newt's stomach made a particularly loud rumbling noise as though in agreement with the squire's request, the evening's plan was decided.

*　　*　　*

"Now this . . . this is a meal!"

Newt and Ailis both raised their mugs to that toast, clinking them in turn against the roasted drumstick Gerard was tearing into. He had declined the weak, watered-down ale that they were drinking, preferring the crystal-cool water that seemed to be the specialty of this town, drawn from the well where they had been sitting earlier.

The tavern was small with barely enough room for the owner to move around the few tables set around a central hearth. There was firewood in it, but because the day had been warm, it was unlit. In the cooler days and nights of winter, though, it would doubtless give off a welcome antidote to the chill.

"What do you think is happening . . . back home?" Ailis asked, after they had taken the edge off their hunger. She had been about to say "back in

91

Camelot," but remembered their story just in time. The other tables were filled with locals, some eating, others simply drinking their fill. From the few snatches of conversation she caught, they all seemed to speak in the baffling manner of the other villagers. Ailis didn't know if that was good or bad. She'd like to think that it had been Merlin giving them a message through the woman, and that they were among loyal friends. But they had no way to know for certain, so they couldn't risk mentioning Camelot—not when the safety of everyone she cared about rested on Arthur's enemies not knowing that for several days now, he had been asleep and not on the throne. The need for the Grail, something she had scoffed at earlier, suddenly made more sense. Even asleep, a Grail King could protect his country, just by the possession of the Grail itself. And maybe it would have deflected the spell in the first place . . . if all the stories were true.

"Every time I try to think about what's happening back there my stomach hurts," she went on. "All the things that—"

"They'll be careful," Gerard said sternly. "And anyway, we can't do anything about it—not until we're home. By then it will be a story to tell."

"We hope," Newt said darkly, biting into his meal with more force than the cooking warranted. Ailis flinched at his words.

"Hope. Yes." Gerard was doing his best Sir Rheynold imitation, confident and paternal, and failing miserably as his voice cracked on the last word. He recovered, then went on. "That's all we can do, isn't it?" The two boys locked stares across the table, both their faces drawn into lines that made them look older than their years.

"It is all we can do," Gerard said again. "Hope . . . and finish our part in this by bringing the owl home to roost."

"Speaking of which . . . it should be almost moonrise."

Newt looked regretfully at the remains of his meal, then pulled a mostly clean cloth out of his pocket and wrapped the meat and a thick slice of bread in it. He placed the entire thing back into his pocket.

"What?" he asked, looking up to see the two of them staring at him. "We paid for it. And it's good."

Ailis's lips twitched, and she reached into the deep pocket of her skirt and pulled out a slightly cleaner cloth and did likewise with her own leftovers. When

Gerard made no move to imitate them, she reached over and gathered up the remains of his meal as well. "You'll be hungry later tonight," she told him.

The conversation with the innkeeper as they settled their bill was as confusing as any they had heard in this town, but Ailis could almost understand the man as he—she thought—wished them a good evening. If this was what extended exposure to Merlin's magic did to you, as Newt suspected, it didn't seem too terrible a price. The people and animals seemed healthy, the town was clean and well kept, and the villagers didn't seem in need of fighters or battlements to protect it. What was a strange manner of speaking in exchange for that?

*   *   *

The sun had gone down below the rooftops by the time they gathered the horses and the mule from the old man, with an extra coin thrown in by Ailis for his honesty in not touching their saddlebags. Gerard frowned when she took the extra coin from the pouch, but didn't say anything.

Tying their bags back onto the saddles and mounting took only a few moments. Soon they were moving down the road through town as the air darkened from dusk into night. Once they were past the town walls, the road widened enough for them to ride three abreast. Trees gave way to fields and the sky spread out over them without interruption.

"So many stars," Ailis noted in wonder. Inside Camelot, a servant was always busy with the things that needed doing. She couldn't remember the last time she had paused just to look up at the sky.

"We're fortunate it's clear," Gerard said, his gaze moving from the sky to the surrounding fields and then back again. He shifted in his saddle, feeling the comforting weight of the sword strapped within easy reach near his leg. Newt had a cudgel he had fashioned from a thick tree branch, and Gerard suspected he could use it at least as well as his fists. But Ailis was unarmed, and the three of them would look like easy pickings to any thief who might be out this evening on this stretch of road.

"And lucky that it's not the new moon," Newt added. "Lucky."

"I don't trust luck," Gerard said. "Too flighty." He caught the look Ailis gave him and added, "Not that I'm ungrateful for it, I just don't want to rely on it."

She seemed satisfied, and he let out a shallow breath. She was only a servant girl, yes, but life was much easier when she wasn't upset.

He wondered what would happen to Ailis when they were grown. Would she still serve at Camelot? Or would she find someone to marry and move away to start her own household? It shouldn't matter . . . and yet, somehow, it did.

He cast a sideways glance at Newt. What would he do when he got older? He was good with horses; Gerard saw that. He had probably been good with the hounds once, too, in order to be moved up to the stables. There were many manor-lords who would pay well for a good stable-master, especially one with ties to Camelot.

He had never thought about servants' lives before. They were just . . . there. Gerard shook his head, trying to dislodge the uneasy feeling such thoughts gave him.

The three had been riding along in silence for a while when Newt reined in his gelding and pointed. "It's rising."

Over the horizon the pale yellow disk of the moon slid through the sky.

"It moves faster than I thought," Gerard said.

"At first. Then it slows down. And sometimes it stays forever in the sky, even after the sun comes back up. And in the summer it shows up even in the afternoon." Newt had obviously spent more time moon-watching than the other two.

"I remember." Ailis was quiet for a moment as they watched the moon climb beyond the distant tree line. "Why?"

Newt looked at Gerard, who focused up into the sky and shrugged. "I don't know. There's a story my nurse used to tell me: The moon is a goddess who has lost her followers, and searches each night for new believers—slowing when she thinks she sees them and speeding up again when they turn their back on her."

"A pretty story, but none of that answers the important question: How do we follow the moon?" Newt asked, returning the conversation back to more practical matters.

"I suppose we could just ride under it," Ailis said doubtfully, shifting a little in her saddle to relieve some of the pressure in her legs. She had ridden often when she was a child, but never for so long and not for many years. But she would sooner have her tongue cut out than complain in front of the boys, who would take any sign of weakness as proof that she should have remained back at Camelot.

"You want to ride off the road and across the fields?" Gerard asked. All three turned to look at the broad expanse of fields. Riding through them would mean riding down the crop that was growing there. Even if they were careful, the horses would be destroying food people might need in the winter. And there might be animal holes or hillocks where, in the dark, a horse could stumble and break its leg.

"Bad idea," Newt said finally, and while Ailis wanted to argue when Gerard nodded his head as well, she gave in. They knew horses, and the road.

"So what then?"

"The road is going in mostly the same direction as the moon," Gerard decided. "We'll follow it for as long as we can. It's not as though we have anything specific to go on anyway. Only a puzzle-rhyme from a madwoman."

"One that matches the information on your stolen map," Newt said, his matter-of-fact tone at odds with the tight expression on his face. Ailis looked from one of them to the other and set her heels into her gelding's side, making him break into a trot that almost shook her out of her saddle. She had never known such boys who disagreed with each other!

"The moon's moving," she pointed out. "We should be, too."

They rode in relative silence for another stretch, each of them deep in their own thoughts. Camelot and the chaos of the Great Hall seemed impossibly far away in the mostly quiet air. The wind touched the trees, the leaves making a faint shimmering noise. Once or twice the sudden cry of something hunting or hunted reached their ears. But otherwise the only noises were the heavy thudding of hooves on packed dirt, the swishing of tails, and the slightly nasal sound of Newt's breathing.

"Oh, look!" Ailis said, broken out of her own thoughts by the sight up ahead. "Isn't that pretty?"

"That" was the reflection of the moon, now at a slanted angle overhead, on the waters of a small lake to their left. The waters were so dark as to seem black, and the silver-white light of the full moon created a reflection that appeared to be almost solid. As they watched, it appeared to sink below the waters, twisting and curving until it formed a bridge just below the surface of the lake.

Gerard and Newt both reined their horses in beside Ailis's to watch the phenomenon.

"It almost doesn't seem real," Newt said.

"It's not," Gerard retorted, but without any heat. The sight was lovely, almost magical in its effect but totally natural . . . merely a trick of the eye.

"Do you suppose—"

Whatever Ailis was going to suppose was lost as a harsh cry and the sound of heavy wings overhead made all three of them duck instinctively. A great owl, its wingspan as far across as Ailis's outstretched arms from fingertip to fingertip, swooped low and continued across the water. The moonlight touched its feathers, turning the grays and browns into silvers and golds, before the bird curved around and flew into the night and disappeared across the lake and out of view.

"By all that's holy," Gerard said, and crossed himself almost without thought.

"Magical," Ailis whispered, still staring as though the bird might return simply because she willed it.

"The owl," Newt said a few beats afterward. "'The owl, lonely flier. Moonlight, water, what you desire.'"

The other two turned to stare at him.

"Do you think—"

"You mean—"

They both spoke at the same time, stopped, looked at each other as though expecting the other to continue, and then started again.

"You mean—"

"You can't mean—"

They both stopped again and stared at Newt. The stable boy shrugged and stared out over the water. No, *into* the water. He urged his horse into motion, heading down the road toward the lake and the moonlight bridge.

If this wasn't the place the woman's riddle had spoken of, he'd eat his saddle.

After a moment, the others followed hard on his gelding's hooves, holding their breath in anticipation of . . . something. They weren't sure quite what.

"Halt!"

Newt had to pull up hard on the reins to avoid running over the figure that appeared in front of them. The apparition was tall, wearing a long dark robe with a hood. For a moment their hearts leapt with the hope that it was Merlin come to meet them.

That hope was dashed as other figures could be seen behind them, seemingly appearing out of the air.

"Bandits," Gerard muttered, his hand instinctively going to his sword's hilt as he silently counted their opponents. Too many. If Newt had been trained to fight, maybe . . .

The horses shifted uneasily, clearly wanting to bolt at this sudden rise in tension.

"I believe this is where you hand over your belongings," the leader of the bandits said, placing his hand on Newt's gelding's neck and moving in close, effectively keeping Newt from pulling any weapon he might have on his person. Gerard swore. Hand moved away from his hilt to rest on his knee. Only a fool fought when there was no hope of winning. Better to use his brain to find an advantage. "Study your opponent," Sir Rheynold always said. Find their weakness and use it.

"Your belongings, if you would, young sirs."

"We have none."

It was an even bet who was more surprised at the clear voice that rang out into the night, the bandits or the trio from Camelot. But Ailis swallowed hard, nudged her horse forward, and kept talking.

"We're as poor as you. Perhaps more so. If you must take something, take my horse. He's not attractive, but he is a very good ride, young, and has no brands on him, unlike the others, so no one could claim you stole him, later on." The two horses the boys had brought with them carried Camelot's mark on their ears, easily identifiable by any knight or noble these bandits might encounter. There's no way to insist upon your innocence when you're riding a beast you have no legal claim to.

"You might be lying," the bandit said thoughtfully.

"We might. But you can see that we are not dressed well, riding at night with no adult to protect us. No jewels. No fancy weapons. And we are very young and not much glory to kill." She put on her very best serious expression, the one the ladies of the court seemed to prefer on those who served them— the proper face, Lady Melisande called it, although she never said proper for what.

It seemed to work on bandits as well, because the leader peered closely at her then laughed.

"You bargain well, little merchant. And I do not want to have the blood of children on my hands." The King's Law was harsh enough on murderers, but those who killed children found no mercy in Arthur's lands. "Your lives are worth . . ." The leader walked around them, casually noting the quality of their horses and confirming that the other two were indeed clearly marked. "Your horse and the mule. And whatever it carries."

"Whatever it carries save our food," Ailis bargained. "Killing children by starvation is no better." Gerard had kept the map on him, and his belongings were tied to his own saddle. Anything she or Newt had placed on the mule could be well lost if it let them live. Hopefully the boys would agree.

The leader waved one hand carelessly, and two of his followers began going through the mule's packs, removing the packets of food and waterskins, first sniffing them to make sure they contained nothing more interesting than watered-down wine.

"Down you get, little merchant," one of the bandits said, appearing by Ailis's side with unnerving silence. His hands were huge, and he lifted her down from the saddle without trouble. She held her breath, thankful that she had tucked up the skirt she wore over her trousers in order to ride, praying that the darkness would keep him from noticing her gender.

"Be good," she said to her horse, patting it on the neck as the bandit led it away. She felt terribly isolated on the ground, and the look Gerard was giving her when he dismounted to take up the discarded foodstuffs made her feel even worse. So when the leader strode toward her, she had to force herself not to run from him, but stand tall, every inch the defiant boy they thought she was.

The other bandits had already disappeared into the darkness with their prizes, barely a word spoken among them. Their silence was more frightening than anything else.

"You." The bandit leader gestured to Newt. "Take up your companion, boy. It's the least you could do." He vanished into the shadows as Newt moved his horse closer, putting out a hand for Ailis to take and pulling her up behind him.

She could feel Newt's back tense when she put her arms around him, but this horse was wider and higher up from the ground than she was used to, and she wasn't going to risk falling—especially since he had the reins. Not that she didn't trust him, but it was a long fall to the hard ground and . . .

She suddenly realized that Gerard was still staring at her with that disbelieving, betrayed expression on his face, clearly visible in the moonlight.

"What?" she asked him. "What was I supposed to do? Let them take everything we had, maybe kill us, too?"

"I wouldn't have—"

"You would have argued, maybe challenged them? And where would that get us, except dead? And no mission, no Merlin. So we've lost one horse and the mule. They let us keep most of the supplies, which they wouldn't have if I hadn't amused them."

Not to mention, which she wasn't going to, what they might have done if they had realized that she was a girl. She shied away from that thought and went on. "You're afraid that with two of us on Newt's horse we'll move too slowly? Do you want me to get down and walk then?"

Neither boy answered. Ailis felt as if they were blaming or, worse, punishing her for their loss of goods. She felt a cold tension burning inside her at their continued silence. It was as though it were consuming everything in its path, leaving her hollow and shaking, caught up in an abyss. Her mouth opened to scald them with her anger, but no more words came out. A tight fist clenched in her chest, making it difficult for her to breathe.

"Let's go," Newt said finally, moving his gelding forward and startling Ailis who wrapped her arms around his waist to stay on. He could jibe at Gerard's pretensions endlessly for the entertainment of it, but seeing Ailis so angry at the other boy made Newt uncomfortable.

"Go?" Gerard repeated stupidly.

"Moon's going to be overhead soon." Newt looked up and the others followed suit. It seemed like hours while they were facing down the bandits, but in truth

it had only been a span of minutes. The moonlight still slanted down onto the water, but the path somehow seemed less solid, more of a dream or an illusion. "If we're going to do this, we'd better do this."

"If the moon goes down before we get across . . ." Ailis started to say. She caught herself, remembering the owl winging over the water. There was no room to question: They had to trust the words the woman spoke—and their own instincts.

"We won't let it. Ride!" Gerard shouted and kneed his stallion toward the lake and the stretch of silvery moonlight that spanned it. Newt's horse followed close behind. Ailis clung to Newt tighter, her hood falling back and her braid flying out behind her like a tail as they ran. Water splashed around the horses' legs. Gerard's ride stumbled, then recovered. The moonlight caught their clothing, the horses' coats, and their tack and turned everything into shadows of itself.

The water moved up to their knees, soaking them through. Gerard was muttering under his breath, while Newt tried to remember what he knew about how well horses, even laden horses, could swim. Ailis merely closed her eyes and buried her face against Newt's back, praying as hard as she

could to whichever gods might be listening. Then the hooves seemed to catch on something, and suddenly they were moving on a flat surface and the waters were falling away from their knees, down to the horses' hocks.

"The moonlight bridge," Ailis whispered.

"What?"

"A story I heard once. The moonlight bridge will give you what your heart desires. . . ."

Gerard was too far ahead to hear, but Newt clearly did not believe her. Because she was a girl, Ailis thought bitterly. For all their sniping at each other, the two boys still listened to each other. But not her.

"There's something else. . . ." She couldn't remember what, though she knew it was important.

She felt Newt shift in the saddle, as though he were turning to look down at the water.

"Dear God," he whispered, and she felt him shift slightly again, the muscles in his back and legs tightening. He seemed to lunge forward and Ailis felt him slipping out of her grasp.

Then she remembered what else she had heard about the moonlight bridge and grabbed for him again, this time desperate for his safety, not her own.

"Don't look. Don't look!" she yelled, her fingers closing over the rough fabric of his trousers, one hand grabbing at his belt to haul him back into the saddle.

"Please, Newt, don't look," she sobbed. She remembered now. "The moonlight bridge gives you a vision of your heart's desire. . . . And those who dive in after it are never seen again."

Maybe they got what they dreamed of. But it wasn't in this world.

"No," Newt gasped. His backside was firmly back in the saddle and his hands were shaky on the reins. He was looking straight ahead now. "I'm not looking. Not looking."

"You saw your heart's desire?" she asked, curiosity momentarily winning out over fear.

But Newt only murmured, "I'm not looking," as if to convince himself.

And then they were all three on the sandy shoreline of an island that had absolutely not been there when they first rode into the lake. Newt let out a long, quavering sigh that Ailis could feel through his entire body. She hugged him tighter, trying to say something—she wasn't quite sure what. Maybe next time he'd listen to her. . . .

Gerard turned his horse to face back the way they had come. Ailis and Newt, reluctantly, followed suit. There was the shore, clear as could be in the night air. As he watched, the moon changed position slightly and the path they had followed shimmered and became only light on the water.

"That was too close," Newt said, watching the bridge disappear. "How're we supposed to get back?"

"Go forward," Gerard said practically. "Look for something on the other side. There may be another bridge."

"Let's worry about that after we find Merlin," Ailis said. "*If* we find Merlin."

Gerard got down off his horse, making a face as his boots squished with the water inside them. The temptation to take them off and drain the water out was great, but he knew better. Beside the fact that wet leather would be unpleasant if not impossible to put back on, the thought of being caught barefoot and therefore vulnerable in unknown territory was something Sir Bors would never forgive. And Gerard had no desire to be used as an example in a future lecture on preparedness. The fact that nobody would ever know, if he didn't say anything, never entered into his mind.

"So where do we start looking?" Newt asked. "Anyone have a brilliant plan? Preferably one that doesn't involve magic, if it's all the same to you two."

Gerard glared, annoyed by the stable boy's continued lack of respect and proper awe for Merlin, if not magic in general, and by the way Ailis's face fell at Newt's words, though she never said anything out loud. Newt was, after all, the one who had understood the riddle and gotten them here. Credit had to be given.

"Up there," Gerard said, pointing to the slight hill at the far end of the sandy ledge they were on.

"Why there?" Newt asked.

"Because there's nothing here," Gerard said as patiently as he could. "So we should go higher, in order to see what else is on this island."

Newt shrugged, placid and sturdy as a carthorse. "All right."

They led the horses, stumbling and cursing a little when the wet shoes slipped on the grassy hill. There was little light now that the moon was beginning to slide down in the sky, and the air was cool, so they were soon shivering as well.

"Almost there," Newt said, dropping back to give Ailis a hand when she lost her balance and almost fell. She resisted taking his offered hand at first, but common sense got the better of her pride. His surprisingly warm fingers closed over hers and tugged her up the last bit of the rise to where Gerard was already standing, looking out over the view.

"What *is* that?" Newt asked. "That" referred to the pulsing gold arc of light off to the left, rising over the trees.

"Magic." Ailis kept her tone even, despite the urge to be sarcastic. The warm glow that the sight created inside her was clearly not shared by her companions. Not everyone reacted the way she did to the presence of magic. Ailis had trouble remembering that, despite Newt's constant muttered comments.

"Which means that's where Merlin is." Gerard, seemingly oblivious to the sight in front of him and to the tension building between Newt and Ailis, tugged on his horse's reins and led it slowly down the other side of the hill.

"More magic. I suppose it was to be expected," Newt said unhappily, right on cue. When Ailis looked sharply at him, he shrugged. "There isn't any magic in the stables. Just honest horses. I miss that." He followed Gerard down the incline, still muttering under his breath.

Ailis stood on the ridge a while longer, watching in awe. The hill sloped down into a grassy plain, without a tree in sight. In the middle of that plain was a small house; a small house with clear walls, a top and bottom, that pulsed with pale blue and gold light.

Magic indeed.

She smiled, her entire face reflecting her elation. King ensorcelled, horse and mule and belongings stolen, traveling while soaked to the skin and with Gerard still angry with her—it still made her feel as though the world was a wonderful place indeed.

FIVE

The source of the light was a structure unlike any the three had ever seen before. Gerard and Newt slowed, leading their horses at a snail's pace. Ailis strode on ahead of them, her braid thumping against her back as she increased her pace.

The glow was, in fact, coming from the house they had seen from the ridge. It was, in many ways, an unexceptional little cottage—four outer walls surrounded four different rooms of equal size. There was minimal furniture inside: chairs, a bed, a table. One room had a fireplace, with a heavy black pot over it, set into one wall. But the hearth was cold and the pot was empty.

Ailis could tell all of this because the walls were clear. As was the furniture. It was like looking into a particularly still pond of clear water and seeing fish dart right next to your hand even though they were out of reach. Only in this case the dark form moving behind the walls wasn't a fish.

"Ah. There you are."

Whatever they had expected to hear from Merlin, it hadn't been that.

He stood in the doorway, looking at them through the clear door. It was thin, barely a finger's width, and was cold to the touch.

"An ice house?" Ailis ran her fingers over the wall, fascinated enough to ignore the light that came from inside and played over her, attracted by her motion.

Merlin shrugged; a careless gesture.

"May we . . . come in?" Gerard asked, uncertain about the protocols of dealing with an enchanter. Ailis, despite her claims of knowing how to communicate sensibly with Merlin, seemed too fascinated by the structure to be any help.

The question made the enchanter laugh. It was a short and bitter noise. "I'd come out if I could."

"You're trapped?" Gerard looked around as though whoever had trapped Merlin might suddenly spring from nowhere at them. "How?"

"Who did it? Is it the same person who cast the

spell on the court?" Ailis asked in dismay. That would make sense, but if the same foe could take both Merlin and Arthur, the three of them might as well give up and go home!

All three of them started asking questions at once. Then their chatter stopped. They were abashed at being so rude to the second-most powerful man in the kingdom.

"My life's never that easy," the enchanter said, running one hand through his black-and-silver hair, leaving it standing on end and sparking brightly with random magic. "No, my lady Nimue is having her fun with me."

The three teenagers stared at him: Gerard in disgust, Newt in amusement, and Ailis in sympathy. Nimue was a name whispered in Camelot—a former student of Merlin's who had enchanted the enchanter, then left him only to return and leave again, proving him no better than any mortal man.

"Oh, dry it up," he said, seeing their looks. "She played me for a fool and I deserve to stay here until I can find my way out." Merlin was clearly out of patience with them already.

"If you're trapped here, you can't help us," Gerard said. "You can't help your king, who is caught in a bespelled sleep, along with all of his court. You can't—"

"Dry it up, I said," Merlin snapped, and even knowing that a magical wall stood between the two of them, Gerard took a step back.

"You know what has happened," Ailis said, stating a fact rather than asking a question.

"I know," Merlin said. "You think your lot is difficult? Thank the stars above that you're not me. . . . And yes, I'm cranky," he added before any of them could say anything. "You try spending your days in an ice house. Your posterior gets cold after a while. That woman has an evil sense of humor."

He looked at the three of them and sighed, the light that always seemed to burn in his eyes fading a little under their worried, helpless stares.

"We have trouble, children. Whoever has done this clearly wishes to stop the Quest from going forward; either that, or it's the most inconvenient timing in history. And I don't trust coincidences."

"Why would anyone want to stop the Quest?" Newt wondered. "Isn't it just a way to get everyone out of Arthur's hair for a while?"

Merlin almost laughed at that. "If that were so, Arthur would have sent all the troublemakers out, rather than his best and brightest. No, youngster, much as I disagree with Arthur about how he is going about this, the Quest is more important than anyone realizes, even Arthur. The Grail is not merely a symbol of rightful kingship."

"The stories are true?" Gerard blinked, his exhaustion melting away with this revelation. "A man who holds the Grail cannot be defeated?"

"Stories have truth at their soul . . . or they die. That story has lived for generations. That fact alone is enough to make it absolutely vital that Arthur hold this Grail."

"Rather than a rebel chieftain," Gerard said.

"Yes. From the Northlands or across the water. Or, the gods defend us, Rome returning to our shores." The enchanter shook his head regretfully. "I can help you, children. But only so far. You're going to have to do this on your own."

"Do what? How are we . . . what are we supposed to do?" Ailis had hoped that Merlin would explain the voice she sometimes heard in her head, the voice that had been so clear in the aftermath of the sleep-spell. She wished he would say something she would be able to understand, and explain it for the others so she would not have to.

The enchanter's usual wry sense of humor, his sly wordplay, was missing. He wasn't smiling here. He wasn't dancing one step beyond the understanding of mere mortals. He looked worried. And distracted.

"Master Merlin?"

He turned to look at her, and then he did muster a smile. "The little servant-maid. Ailis, yes?"

"Yes." He remembered her name. Was that a good thing or a bad thing? With enchanters one could never tell.

"Good. You're here. I couldn't remember if you would be or not. Smart little girl. Too smart, but you're going to need that."

Ailis opened her mouth to follow up on that, her need to know if he was the one speaking to her finally overpowering all her other fears, but Merlin had moved on.

"And so you'd be the horse-boy." That he said to Newt, who inclined his head guardedly, not sure if he should admit to anything where Merlin was concerned.

"Good. All three here as they need to be." His eyes focused on them again, meeting their gazes, each in turn. "Listen carefully and look carefully, and remember, because I can only share this with you once.

"Listen, children." His voice became hypnotic, his eyes darker, his face more stern; the frustrated, mortal man disappearing once more under the deep water of the enchanter Merlin. "Remember. At the cost of your souls, *remember*."

His long, slender fingers moved, conjuring flame out of air, and the flame etched letters in the ice wall between them:

INTO THE MOMENT
SLIDES THE MOMENT
THE MOMENT SHATTERED
ONE INTO THREE
RECLAIMED BY THREE WHO ARE ONE
AND ONE WHO IS NONE
THREE TO BE CLAIMED
BEFORE THE MOMENT TURNS AT HOME

"Do you have it, children?"

"I think so," Gerard said, while the other two squinted at the letters, frantically trying to memorize the words as the flame started to flicker and fade. It sounded like the riddles the villagers spoke in. Maybe Newt was right about why they spoke that way. If Merlin spent a lot of time around them, the way the map suggested . . .

"Don't think! Know! You must remember. You must know. You are the sole and only hope our kingdom has."

"Us?"

Merlin smiled crookedly at him, the majesty of his magical self dispersing and leaving only a man trapped in a house of ice. "Nobody else has shown up; looks like it will have to be you, fates save us all.

"But beware." He stared at each of them in turn and, mortal or not, his dark eyes pierced them into their hearts. "There is very little time. Arthur needs you, and he needs you to return within seven days."

"Seven—" Gerard started, then shut his jaw and thought. "Seven days from when it happened, or seven days from now?"

"Seven from the midnight of their sleeping. Seven is a magical number. Would have been easier if it had been fourteen or twenty-one, but that's magic for you, never considerate . . ." Merlin's voice trailed off, his gaze went elsewhere, and then he came back to them with a sharp snap.

"Repeat it, children. Repeat it together."

It was awkward, each of them remembering the words in a different rhythm, but by the third line they were speaking in unison:

"Into the moment
slides the moment
the moment shattered
one into three
reclaimed by three who are one
and one who is none
three to be claimed
before the moment turns at home."

Merlin nodded and the light came back into his eyes a little. "Good. Good. You have the map?"

The three looked at each other, almost but not quite beyond wonder that he would know about that as well. Gerard retrieved the map, unrolled it, and held it up so that Merlin could see it.

"Good lad." He put his hand to the wall, and Gerard, acting on some unspoken command, placed the map against his side of the wall as well, so that all three—palm, ice, and map—were touching. There was a shimmer of sparks, almost too brief to see, and then Merlin took his hand away. "Oh, Arthur, you idiot, did you really think a map like this would work?"

"It did," Ailis said, greatly daring. "We used it to find you."

Merlin barked out a laugh. "All right, yes, it did. This one time, it did. But you were lucky. Lucky beyond all belief. The gods had a hand in this, and that always worried me. Never trust the gods, children. Trust yourselves. Trust each other. But trust no gods. They have their own agendas."

"But, Master Merlin, what does it mean—the riddle? What are we supposed to do?" In his urgency, Gerard overrode Ailis's attempt to ask Merlin something. He needed *specifics*. A riddle was nonsense and magic was beyond his understanding. He knew how to hit things, how to ride horses, how to speak well to his betters, and protect those weaker than himself. He didn't know what to do with this.

"Three talismans, squire of Sir Rheynold. Find three talismans that will revoke what has been done. There is no more time to waste. Leave me to deal with this magic that binds me, and quest your own quest. Now go. Go!"

And with that, Merlin turned his back on them and paced to the other side of his ice-cased prison and stared out into the darkness, his hands folded in front of him, his proud features lifted to the night sky. Their conversation was over. He had nothing more to tell them.

A long moment of stunned and hurt silence passed, then Merlin heard the three youths whispering to each other, followed by the sound of them mounting their animals and riding away slowly.

"The gods laugh at me," he said morosely when the last noise of their passing had faded. "Children. Why," the enchanter wondered, "does it always end up with the children?"

From the air around him, Nimue's voice laughed at him, a warm silver chime that could still stir his blood and make him do foolish things. "Because, dear teacher, they're the only ones who will forever look for you. They are the only ones who will believe it can be done."

SIX

"Once, just once, I'd like to hear a story that starts 'And the enchanter told them exactly what to get, and where to get it, and what sort of dangers they would face along the way.'" Newt was grousing again.

"It doesn't happen that way," Ailis said from her perch behind him in the saddle.

"Well, it should. Not all the time, because those would be boring stories. But just this once."

If Gerard hadn't been so frustrated he would have laughed. Newt was sulking like a five-year-old. From the expression on Ailis's face, she was having the same reaction to the stable boy's irritation. The way Newt seemed determined to hate anything that took him out of his ordinary, familiar routine was starting to become more amusing than annoying.

When the three left Merlin in his cage of ice, they had no idea where to go or how to get back across the lake. But they hadn't ridden for more than a few minutes before a spiral of light left the house and followed them.

"Merlin's doing?" Newt asked warily.

Ailis stared at the light and shrugged, tucking her braid back under her collar so it wouldn't hit her back so annoyingly when she rode. "Maybe. Maybe not. If not, it would be Nimue's work, and for all that she's a thorn in Merlin's side, she's never acted against anyone else. She's loyal to the king. And considering we don't have any other guides stepping forward . . ."

The light moved ahead of their horses, and the three companions let it lead them away from the house of ice and toward the south through a grove of pines.

The moon had set, and with it, full darkness fell over the island. They slept under the pines on a bed of soft needles for a few hours, feeling oddly protected.

*   *   *

They woke with the first rays of dawn sunlight coming though the trees; their guide-light had disappeared. When they emerged on the other side of the grove, they were back on the road where they had met the bandits, back where they had started before riding into the lake.

"Magic," Newt said again. Gerard clouted him on the shoulder and asked him if he would have rather swum across the lake, or perhaps gone back to the ice house and told Merlin that they were sorry but they couldn't carry out the quest he had given them and oh, well, so much for Camelot. That had almost started a rematch of the stable fight, but Ailis grabbed a hank of Newt's hair and dragged him aside, and then stared at Gerard.

"Don't be an idiot," she told him acerbically, and he backed down.

But now they had to decide what they were going to do, which led to more arguments, not only over the what, but the how.

"We don't even know what the talismans are!" Newt had dug his heels in, not wanting to go farther without a definite plan and destination. He had suggested returning to Camelot, in order to search for a clue as to who their enemy was.

"We don't have time to waste. Merlin said so." Any doubts Gerard might have had about the enchanter had disappeared, mainly because they didn't have any other option but to trust him. "We've already used two days, not knowing. We only have five more left including today. And sitting here arguing is merely using up the time we have left."

"Gerard is right. There's nothing back home that can help us—even if we knew where to begin looking through Merlin's library—don't you think he would have sent us back there if the answers could be found that easily?"

Newt stubbornly set his jaw but couldn't come up with any new arguments.

"So we go forward," Ailis continued. "We need to think of where we should look."

"No. First we need to know what we're looking for! Newt is right about that, although I hate to admit it. We need to figure out the riddle, not blindly trust that we'll stumble on further clues."

Ailis picked up the end of her braid and started to tug at it as she thought out loud. "All those lines about moments . . . The talismans must have something to do with time."

"Time . . . and the turning of time. The stopping of time." Newt was just tossing words around to see what felt right together.

"A sundial?" Gerard asked, dubious.

"How could a sundial be a talisman? They're

huge stone things, I've seen one. We have to be able to take it with us! Don't we?" Newt looked at the other two, his eyebrow raised in question.

"I think so," Ailis said slowly. "We need to bring all three talismans back to Camelot to break the spell. That's how it works in all the stories."

"So a water clock would be right out, then."

"The map," Gerard said suddenly. "Where did I put the map?" He scrambled for his pack, pulled out the tube, and unrolled the map. "When Merlin touched it he did something to it I think."

They gathered around the map, now spread out on the ground. This time it stayed unrolled on its own.

"Look! That's where the island was! And here—" Ailis touched a part of the map with one fingertip, then pulled her hand back in surprise when that portion of the map started to glow.

"What is it doing?" Gerard asked uneasily.

"Glowing?"

That got Newt a look from both Ailis and Gerard, and he shrugged helplessly in return. "Well, it *is*."

"It's glowing where we are," Ailis identified the cause. "But that's not much help. Still . . . Merlin wouldn't have done whatever he did if it wasn't going to be useful. He did whatever he could to help us." Ailis was certain of that.

"You think the map will show us where to go?"

"That would be a nice change," Newt said, but his tone was softer than before.

"Keep it out," Ailis directed Gerard.

"It's too big. It will rip. Or get ruined."

Ailis looked at him, then scooped up a handful of mud and tossed it. Gerard ducked, and it landed smack in the middle of the map.

"Hey!" Then he looked. "Hey. . . ."

The mud slid off the map when he picked it up, leaving no trace of dirt behind.

"If he was going to magic it, he would make sure it wouldn't be easily ruined. Like the Round Table, which they say never needs dusting."

Gerard was clearly annoyed that he hadn't thought of that first. "Fine. I'll keep it out. But that still doesn't tell us where we should start looking."

"Hold it out in front of you," Newt suggested.

"Open?" Gerard looked at the map, which was as wide across as he could spread his arms, and then looked back at Newt as though the other boy had gone mad.

"No, rolled up inside out. So we can see the marks on it—see if it does anything. Go a little one way, then a little another way."

"And if it starts to glow—"

"We go that way," Newt said, finishing Gerard's thought. For once, all three were in perfect agreement.

Retracing their steps had no effect, but a foray down the road to where it split into two smaller lanes caused that area of the map to emit the faintest pale pink glow, like the moment before sunrise, and taking the left-hand turn made the glow darken to a deep rose color. But when they turned the two horses in that direction, the map faded back to its original, ordinary, unglowing self.

"Wonderful." Gerard stared at the map as though expecting it to apologize. Newt drew a deep breath as though he were about to make another comment about the uselessness of magic. Fed up, Ailis reached from her position behind Newt and grabbed the map out of Gerard's hands. It felt warm to the touch, like something living. Her fingers tightened around it instinctively.

"Magic's not a cure-all. Haven't you been paying any attention at all?" Some of this anger was directed at herself, she knew. Part of her had expected Merlin to come back with them and set everything right. She knew what he could do. She had been closer than any of them to the workings of the castle—she had heard all the gossip from the household servants and the queen's ladies alike. And Merlin had given them what help he could. Still, she should have asked the question that had been gnawing at her. Something was changing inside Ailis.

She had heard that voice more than once, and she had begun to feel an affinity for everything that was magic. She had no idea if that was good or bad, helpful or dangerous. Ailis didn't dare mention these thoughts to the boys, especially Newt. She didn't know how Newt would react at all. He didn't like magic. But she thought maybe he liked her. And . . . she didn't want to risk changing that.

Anyway, magic wasn't just a thing, like a sword. It couldn't be handed off, no matter what gifts Merlin gave them, no matter what voices she heard in her head. None of that would change the fact that when they ran into something that three teenagers, two horses, and one sword couldn't handle—and there was no question that they would—it was going to be bad.

*   *   *

The next morning saw the three teens riding through a patchwork of fields and small, weather-beaten structures. There were people working in the fields, men and women wearing brown tunics bent over the crops, but they didn't look up when the two horses went by.

"That's odd," Gerard said. "When Sir Rheynold and I ride in from his lands—"

"You're carrying his banner, better dressed, and riding better horses," Newt said bluntly. "We look like the tail end of a long journey, and not one well started, either. No reason for them to take note of us."

"Still. I don't like it." But the buildings were in good repair, and the workers looked well-fed and healthy, and if they had no curiosity about strangers riding through, then what affair was it of his? Though it did not bode well for asking questions if the workers took no notice of what was around them. Perhaps the master of these lands would be able to give them the information they sought.

The trio passed by a neatly tended farmhouse, but when Gerard stopped to ask an old woman pulling water from a well where they might find a place to stay, she looked at him wide-eyed, like a frightened horse, and told him, in a soft tone he almost couldn't hear, to "go to the Grange."

The Grange, as it turned out, was the largest, best-cared-for farm in the community. The main house was a sturdy structure of stone and wood, two stories high, and the cattle grazing about it looked well-fed and strong.

"The map's glowing," Gerard said suddenly.

"Much?" Ailis asked.

"Just a little."

"Put it away. Quickly!" They didn't know who their enemy was. They couldn't trust anyone. But with luck, their first talisman was within reach. As an afterthought, Gerard took off his leather surcoat, with its identifying mark of Sir Rheynold's household, and put it away, too. The master of the Grange might be educated enough to identify it.

Riding into the yard, they were met by a servant who welcomed them in the name of the master, Daffyd, son of Robert, and offered them cool water. Gerard drank deeply—to do otherwise would have been insulting to the Grange's hospitality. Ailis took a more shallow sip, while Newt barely touched his lips to the rim of the jar, swallowing dramatically as though he had taken a gulp. Hospitality was hospitality, and if they were to ask questions—and get answers—they had to win their host's trust and respect. But Newt didn't know that there was any need to be foolish about it, not with so much weighing on the successful conclusion of their quest.

"Ah, young gentles, welcome!" The master of the Grange was a square-shaped, sly-faced man, ruddy-skinned and dark-haired, with odd blue eyes that were too sharp for his open-handed actions. Newt was reminded of a dog he'd worked with once years ago. Excellent bloodlines, but it had a nasty streak a mile wide. You'd think it was tame to the hand, and then it would turn and savage you.

He was very glad now that he hadn't swallowed any of this man's water. Not that he thought Daffyd, son of Robert, would poison them . . . but you never thought that dog would attack, either.

"How may I help you, young gentles?"

"Board for the night, if you might have the space," Gerard said. "A hot meal would be welcome as well."

The landowner smiled wide at them, and Newt thought there might have been sharp edges on his teeth. "And for this boarding? Will you do a day's work for me?"

Gerard stopped, caught off guard. He had never

been asked for payment before. Occasionally, when Sir Rheynold left, there would be a touch of the hand, coins exchanged, but it was in the way of thanking, not required in advance. Newt was right. This was very different from what he was accustomed to. He didn't know what to say in response.

"We will work for our board," Ailis said, praying her lighter tone would pass for that of a beardless boy. "Half a day's worth is fair bargain." Her encounter with the bandits had given her the confidence to try and haggle. The bandits could have killed them, or worse. All this man could do was send them away. "I have training in the kitchens. My companions are trained to work the stables."

The farmer stared at her, then at the boys. "I do not need kitchen work nor stables. But my fields are rich this season, and I have not enough workers to toil there. Fair trade, shelter and sustenance for a day's work?"

"Half a day," Gerard said. They needed information, a chance to investigate the map's message, but they could not risk spending more time here if there was nothing to be gained.

"Half a day, then," the master agreed. "But for now, come! Your horses will be well cared for while we determine where you will best earn your keep here."

The three of them dismounted and handed their reins to the servant who had offered them the water. Before they were led away, Gerard lifted the saddlebag with the map off its hook and draped it over his shoulder, his expression daring anyone to say something about it.

Nobody did.

*   *   *

"I would rather be in the kitchens," Ailis said, "with Cook in a bad mood."

Gerard was too tired to respond.

They were weeding: Tiny green sprouts were to be protected, while the equally tiny but differently shaped green sprouts next to them were to be pulled and tossed into the sacks they'd been issued. Hours ago Gerard had given up trying to tell the difference and was taking the weeds Ailis pulled and putting them into his sack. Freed from having to carry one herself, she was able to work quickly enough to not bring down the wrath of the man Newt had immediately dubbed the slave master, who stalked the sides of the field looking for workers who seemed to be slowing down.

The Grange servants seemed to fall into two categories: stolid, silent types who handled their baskets and hoes with the casual skill that came from years of practice, and more sullen-looking workers, who hacked at the ground indifferently. Neither type was particularly friendly, although Gerard admitted that he didn't have much experience with servants at this level. Perhaps it was entirely normal. He thought about asking Ailis, but she had always worked in the castle under much gentler conditions. She likely wouldn't know either.

Newt might know, but he had separated from them early on, joining forces with another weeder, and was now working in another section of the field. Occasionally they would see him stand and stretch, casually looking around to make sure they were still within eyesight. But there was no opportunity to speak with him.

"Care to place a wager that Master Daffyd"—and Gerard made the title an insult—"has gone through our belongings?"

"Or had his servants do it. They give me the shivers, some of them. Their eyes are dead. Have you noticed? Like there's no one inside. Ugh." Ailis shuddered at the thought, then said, "The map?"

Gerard inclined his head to the saddlebag, which he had brought with him, defying any of the locals to make a comment. "Is safe. I wasn't going to trust it out of my sight."

Ailis stopped, her hand closing around a particularly stubborn weed. "Do you think—"

"I didn't like the look in his eyes," Gerard said, putting his hand around hers and yanking. The weed came up, knocking them both on their backsides.

"Thank you ever so much, brave Sir Weed Killer." Ailis made as though to curtsey, impossible in her rough trousers, and stopped only when she realized how odd that would look to anyone who might be watching. It wasn't the big things, like lowering her voice or passing water privately, that made pretending to be a boy so tricky. Small things were what caught you out, every time. If only it were acceptable for girls to travel like this; boys had the freedom to!

"Very. Funny." Gerard sat up, decided that only his dignity had been injured, and wiped the dirt off his hands. "I know that there is no work without its own worth, but this is an experience I would have gladly gone without."

A low chuckle from behind made both of them start and look around.

"There are worse jobs, youngster. There are many worse jobs."

The speaker was an older man, his face lined from years in the sun, his silver hair pulled back into a knot at the back of his neck.

"Perhaps." Gerard tossed the weed into his bag, and offered his hand to the stranger. How much had this old man heard? He made a resolution to be more careful, minding his speech. "I'm Gerard."

The older man looked at his hand, then shook his head and took up the hand clasp. "Beren." He looked at Ailis, and she nodded her head shyly, rubbing her hand on the side of her trousers as though to clean them, but actually spreading more dirt over them to disguise the slenderness of her fingers. "Aili," she said, giving her childhood nickname which could have belonged to a boy or a girl.

"You're new here." It wasn't a question. "Old Daffyd hired ye for the season?"

"We're only passing through," Gerard said, nudging Ailis so that she started weeding again. They had wanted to talk to people, yes, but there was no reason to attract unwanted attention by seeming to slack off on their work. "Just paying for a night's room and board."

"Passing through, are you?" Beren looked at them carefully then shrugged. "No concern of mine," he said, almost to himself. "Offered you shelter, did he?"

"Yes. Why?"

"Nah, nah, nothing. Only best be careful where you lay your head."

"We're almost done," Gerard said. "Half a day was our agreement. So we'll be gone soon."

Beren's expression at that made Gerard wary. "Is there something you want to tell us?" the squire asked as he took the weeds from Ailis's hand and tossed them into the sack.

Beren shook his head, retreating from his earlier friendliness. "On your own, you are. As we all are." And he would say no more.

Ailis and Gerard exchanged worried glances but had no choice but to go back to work.

* * *

"You smell." Newt knelt on the rough wooden floor and began to remove his shoes.

"So do you." Gerard tossed his clothing into a pile and used a ragged towel to wipe himself off. There had been limited water offered for them to

141

bathe with when they came in from the fields. Ailis had looked so pitiful, the two boys had agreed without speaking to let her have it all. They could hear her now, behind a hastily erected screen, splashing and humming. By the time they had finished dressing, the noises had stopped and she came around the screen, dressed, with her hair laying wet over her shoulders and her face scrubbed pink.

Gerard looked longingly at the thin pallets they had been given. A far cry from his bed back home, but right now it was worth a solid gold piece to him, if he could only lie down for an hour or five. But they had been invited to meet with the master of the Grange before the midday meal. From the way Newt's stomach had been growling, Gerard didn't think either of his companions was going to like that bit of news.

"I feel so much better," Ailis declared, braiding her hair up again. "I feel I could take on anything right now."

"Well, that's good. Because we're about to." Newt and Ailis turned in confusion to look at Gerard. "A servant stopped me on the way up. Daffyd wants to see us, personally, before we go down to dinner."

"So?"

Gerard shook his head, exasperated by Newt's

question. "The map said that one of the talismans was here, didn't it?"

"It glowed. We still don't know what that means. It could just mean that we're moving in the right direction. Or that someone here has information we need. Or . . . anything!"

Gerard considered that. "Even if Daffyd does have the first talisman, how will we know what it is? It could be anywhere. It could be anything. If we could figure out some way to question him—"

"That assumes he'd be willing to help us, and that we could believe what he says," Ailis pointed out. "I don't think he's to be trusted."

"He's not," Newt agreed. "I spoke with some of the workers. They would not speak ill of the man."

Ailis shook her head. "How does that—"

"There's no slave so well-treated that he will not speak ill of his master. The only man who is silent is one who's afraid."

"So speak carefully," Gerard interrupted. "Better yet, don't speak at all. Let me talk to him."

"What? You don't think we can—" Ailis started, her expression indignant.

"No. I don't. Come on, Ailis. Think for a moment. You didn't even want him to know you were a girl.

The minute you start to talk for any length of time, he'll know. You think he'll listen to you then? And Newt—"

"I'm not ashamed of who I am," Newt retorted.

The squire threw his hands up in frustration. "I'm not saying you are. But I know men like this Master Daffyd. They're proud. The way he treated us, like we'd agree to whatever he said just to get fed? You said it yourself, Newt—we weren't impressive. If we had been—if I'd ridden in here with Sir Rheynold—he'd have been all over us like a dog hoping for a bone." Gerard shook his head. "I'm not trying to be cruel, honestly. But the only way to talk to someone like this is from a position of strength. And neither of you can do that."

"You just spent half the day digging weeds. What makes you think he's going to recognize you as any better than us?" Ailis meant the words to sting, and they did.

"I have a better chance than either of you." But Gerard's voice, previously confident, began to waver a little with doubt. The sight of the servants slogging back from the field, half of them without any animation or casual talk at all, had unnerved him more than he would admit.

"We're doomed." Newt sat down on the one stool in the room and put his head in his hands. "And I'll never get my supper."

*   *   *

The moment they entered Daffyd's study, Newt felt the unease he'd experienced before jump in intensity. A sideways glance showed that Ailis was equally nervous, if the way she kept rubbing her hands flat against her shirt was any indication. Almost in passing, Newt noticed that when she did that, the fabric pulled tight across her chest. He hadn't noticed before, much, but they were going to have to find her a jacket or vest of some kind if she was going to keep passing as a boy.

"Ah . . . ready to be on your way, are you?"

Daffyd sat in a heavy chair, his back to the one window in the room. The sun came through at such an angle that he seemed almost surrounded by the late afternoon light. If you looked directly at him, you had to squint or risk being blinded. Newt had seen better in bit-player shows. But this was Daffyd's ground, and that made him worth watching. Even if that idiot Gerard didn't seem to realize it, bulling forward with bluster wasn't going to win the day.

"We thank you for your hospitality. But yes, after

the midday meal we will be ready to be on our way."

Newt had to admit, the way the words dripped off the other boy's lips, you'd think he was Arthur himself being gracious to unworthy underlings. An annoying twit, yes, but a well-trained annoying twit. Gerard was almost as good as he thought he was.

"Not so quickly, my young sirs," Daffyd said, stretching his legs out in front of him.

Newt tensed. He didn't like the sound of that. Not at all.

"I have a challenge for you. A game of sorts, if you will."

"And if we won't?" Newt asked quietly under his breath.

Daffyd went on without hearing him. "I have in this room my most valuable possession. If you can tell me it true, it is yours."

Ailis looked at Newt, then at Gerard. Newt looked back at them blandly, not showing his unease on his face. It felt like a trap somehow. Adults didn't simply make offers like that, not to random travelers and especially not to young travelers without status.

Ailis spoke for them all. "And if we cannot tell you what that possession is?"

Daffyd smiled, and Newt was certain he saw

sharp teeth this time. "Then you stay and work my lands." And with those words, the three could feel the weight of something falling around them, sealing them into the room.

"Excuse us a moment?" Gerard said, taking his companions by the arm and leading them a short distance away, out of their host's hearing.

"I don't like this," Newt said.

"I *really* don't like it," Ailis said in a small voice. "He stinks." The two boys looked at her, and she clarified, "Of magic. Can't you—" No, they couldn't, clearly, despite it being so obvious to her. "I can smell it on him in here. This entire room. Magic. Of a darker sort than anything I've ever felt from Merlin. If we agree, we'll be bound by the terms. We'll end up like half the workers in the fields, the ones with the dead eyes."

"You think they're bound by magic? Daffyd is using magic to control his Grange?" He looked at Newt, who nodded, remembering the strange weight in the room when they came in. "Then the King needs to know about this!"

"To tell him, we've got to escape first," Newt pointed out. "I say we decline his offer and pass on dinner as well. Once we get away, we can try and figure out what to do about the map glowing."

"Agreed," Gerard said. His face was pale with anger, not fear.

Behind them, the door opened. Two large men stepped inside, short swords strapped to their waists, clearly there to enforce the rules of Daffyd's surprise game.

The three companions looked at each other: Newt unsurprised, Ailis afraid, Gerard furious.

"This is your hospitality?" Gerard demanded. "Armed guards to force us into a bargain we have not agreed to?" He might have sounded impressive if his voice hadn't cracked halfway through. Still, he stood his ground, glaring at Daffyd.

"My boy. There have been no threats made." But the threat was implicit in the way the two guards stood.

Gerard growled like one of the hounds from the kennel, then turned to his companions. "We each get a chance, that should—"

"No." Daffyd shook his head with mock sorrow. "One request, one agreement, one chance. Those are the rules."

"That's not fair," Ailis protested.

Newt snorted. "Nothing about this is fair. Nothing about any of this has been fair."

Gerard nudged Ailis and got Newt's attention as well. They moved away from both Daffyd and his guards. "Look around," he said in a tight whisper.

"What?" Newt kept his voice low as well, but they could all hear the fear in it.

"Look around this room," he said again, still whispering. "The map. It's glowing."

"How can you tell?" As far as they could see, it was still tucked into his back, safely out of sight.

"I can feel it. It was warm before, but it's almost hot, now. Almost . . . almost as if it knew I couldn't see it and wanted to be sure it got my attention."

"You think the talisman is in here?"

Gerard's scorn won through the anger he was feeling about the trap they found themselves in. "Any other reason the map might be glowing, horse-boy?"

"I haven't any idea." Newt put his hands on his hips and glared at Gerard, wanting nothing more than to knock him down again and wipe that look off his face once and for all. He caught the guards staring at him and lowered his voice again. "It's all magic . . . and I'm tired of it."

"Well, don't be. It might be the only thing that saves us," Ailis snapped. "Merlin put his magic into the map," she reminded them with a bit more patience. "So if the map is getting warm now, it must be reacting to something in this room. It's Merlin helping us as much as he can. That's what he meant when he said he couldn't help us directly. He has to work through the map."

"So if the talisman is in here," Gerard said in an undertone, "wouldn't that be Daffyd's most valuable possession? Do you really think he'll let us walk out of here with it?"

"He *has* to if we find it," Ailis insisted. "His own magic should bind him to his side of the deal, the same as it binds us. But we need to find the talisman first. And we have no idea what it looks like."

"Then we'd better start looking," Newt said, but his voice didn't sound like he had much hope of success.

The three of them separated and walked around the room as though deep in thought over their predicament, carefully avoiding getting too close to the two guards by the door.

The study itself was unremarkable, a farmer's hodgepodge of bits and ends: bags of seed in one corner, ledgers on a narrow shelf, and a pile of harnesses tossed in another corner. The floor was scuffed from wear, and the only furniture other than the chair Daffyd sat in like a throne was a battered wooden table covered with more ledgers and parchments. It was prosaic and ordinary and boring, and no place you would think to find a magical talisman that would help free a king from enchanted slumber.

Newt walked slowly, trying to pretend that he was deep in thought while his gaze scanned every surface, every handspan of the room. It had to be in here. Not because he believed Gerard's stupid map, but because if it wasn't, he had no idea what they'd do next. He wasn't going to become a slave in all but name for this madman of a farmer, that was for sure! And he wouldn't let Ailis end up here, either. The thought of abandoning Gerard to his fate was tempting, but Newt quickly discarded it. He didn't like the oh-so-proud squire any better than when he had knocked the snot out of him four days earlier, but it would take all three of them to even have a chance of escaping this room. Once they'd gotten free, they'd have to abandon the horses. It pained him, but he knew the animals would be treated well here—good horses were more valuable than people, especially if you used slaves—and the surprise factor of not trying for the stables might ultimately buy them some time.

On the other hand, trying to go on foot would slow

them down horribly. Even if they found the talisman here, they'd still have two more to find and—counting the rest of this day—only four days left to do it.

Newt ran the plan over again in his head, trying out all the possible angles. It had about as much chance as a goose in Cook's huge hands, but he'd yet to see a goose give up without a fight. He looked up, meaning to try and catch Gerard's eye, when something caught his attention.

There. In the far corner of the room, in a jumble of junk. He frowned, trying to determine why he was looking there. It was nothing. Just a . . .

He frowned again. What *was* that? A goblet of some sort? Glass, clearer than the rough-blown versions normally seen around Camelot: wide and rounded at the bottom, but lengthening and narrowing at the top, with a tiny mouth. And it was small, barely the size of two hands clenched together.

Whatever it was, it was . . . glowing. Faintly. Barely even noticeable; barely even there, unless you were looking with eyes that had seen too much magic for comfort. Tiny blue sparkles around it were similar to what had come from Merlin's hand when he touched the map. That alone gave Newt the confidence to move toward it.

The closer he got, the more intense the flickers became until he was amazed that nobody else was jumping forward to grab it. A quick glance backward showed that the two guards were oblivious so long as nobody went near the door, and Daffyd was watching Gerard. So the squire had been right about how Daffyd would react, if not in the way he thought. Ailis had been conferring with Gerard, their heads bent together, red to blond. But while Newt watched them she looked up as though sensing his attention. He let his gaze flick from them to the talisman—what he *hoped* was the talisman—and then back again. Her eyes widened slightly, and she nodded, then reached out to touch Gerard's hand as though continuing their discussion.

Gerard then picked up a tarnished metal tankard and turned toward Daffyd, distracting him further, while Ailis walked slowly to join Newt on the other side of the room.

"You see it?"

"Yes." She moved forward, as though drawn on a string, and reached out to lift the talisman from the junk surrounding it. "It's beautiful." Her voice was soft with amazement.

"What is it?"

"I don't know. But . . . it feels warm." They were whispering, but there was no need. Daffyd was still watching Gerard, and the guards were watching Daffyd, waiting mindlessly for his signal.

"Like the map?"

"I . . . don't know. I suppose." Her fingers were stroking the glass the way she might a kitten, examining and protecting at the same time. The sparks seemed to flow into her skin and then back out into the glass, slowly fading the longer she held it.

"You're stalling, Gerard." Daffyd's voice carried across the room. His tone was still jovial, but the blade was no longer hidden. "Give me your guess. Or pay the forfeit."

"This," Ailis said, holding up the glass object, her fingers curved around the widest end. Daffyd turned to look at them with satisfied anticipation.

But his expression faltered and broke as the blue sparks flared again, deeper and darker and more brightly than before, almost as though taunting Daffyd's disbelief.

"Impossible!"

The guards stirred at his outburst but, seeing no physical mayhem, did nothing more than glare suspiciously at the trio.

Daffyd stood, his entire body radiating a palpable menace. There was no more landed farmer—he was every inch the bandit, more so than the ones who had robbed them by the lakeside. "Give that to me!"

"No." Gerard stepped forward, getting between the farmer and the talisman. "You said we could have your most valuable possession if we guessed it. We've guessed it. It's ours."

"He didn't know," Ailis said. "He didn't even know what his most valuable possession was! That's why no one has ever escaped him, because even if they found what he thought was most valuable, it wasn't. He was thinking in terms of what was impor-tant to *him*, probably something costly, not what was valuable in and of itself. The talisman has been here, all the time, but he thought it was junk. But the magic knew that somehow, it was the most valuable thing he owned!"

"Silence!" Daffyd roared. Ailis inched back, but her hold on the talisman remained steady. Gerard stepped into the blast of the man's anger, his shoulders squared and firm as though he were readying a lance for a joust.

"Your own magic betrays you," he said, and even the faint squeak in his voice didn't faze him. "No matter what you thought or believed, it doesn't matter. Your words bind you, as they bind us, and now you must abide by them. Let us go."

Daffyd scowled terribly, his predator's smile a true grimace now, but Gerard stood firm. Newt put a hand on Ailis's elbow and, without discussion, the three of them began the short walk toward the door, the talisman sheltered in the crook of Ailis's arm.

They could smell the somewhat musty odor of the guards' bodies rising off their skin before Daffyd barked out a command, and the two men stood aside, letting them exit without harm.

They walked down the short hallway without seeing anyone and were outside in the courtyard before any alarm was raised.

"Praise the gods," Ailis whispered, but Newt merely tightened his grip on her arm.

"We're not safe yet," he said. "I'm going to go get the horses." If the guards didn't move, if Daffyd really was bound by his own spell . . . they had a chance, if everything played out well. And if not . . ."You two, start down the road like you're walking away. Just do it!"

They looked like they wanted to argue, but Newt turned and started walking slowly, casually toward the stables before they could say anything.

"Come *on*," Gerard said when Ailis hesitated. "Come *on*. He can handle the horses. We need to get out of here."

They had taken their belongings with them, not trusting their safety, so there was nothing to do but put one foot in front of the other until they were out of the shadow of the Grange, back on the main road, out in the deepening shadows of the afternoon.

"Walk faster," Gerard said, stretching his own legs now to cover more ground.

"But Newt—"

"Will be riding. Stop worrying about him!"

They increased their pace, watching the workers in the fields out of the corner of their eyes, alert for even a hint of an alarm. But the workers remained bent over the crops, intent on their work. Gerard felt the weight of shame drape over him for running away like this. A knight was supposed to rescue those in need and certainly anyone trapped by Daffyd's spell deserved to be freed. But . . . he wasn't a knight. Yet. They had barely escaped themselves. How could he help anyone else?

"When this is over," he promised them, even though they couldn't hear, "we'll come back. Arthur himself will break that spell and free you."

There was a hollow thudding noise behind them before Ailis could respond, and Newt arrived, riding his own horse and leading Gerard's and a third by the reins.

"You stole a horse?" Gerard was horrified.

"I borrowed it," Newt said. "We'll make better time if we're all mounted. Besides, I think she has a fascination for your noble steed."

In fact, the mare did seem attached to Gerard's horse, staying close to him as they waited for their riders to mount. With a glance at Newt, Ailis took the reins from him and swung herself into the saddle of the dark brown mare. The saddle was uncomfortable, but the beast seemed to have a sweet enough mouth, and after a flick of one delicate ear, she responded well to Ailis's commands.

Gerard stopped long enough to take the talisman and wrap it carefully in a length of cloth, securing it safely before swinging himself up and into his own saddle.

"One talisman captured," he said with satisfaction, gathering up the reins and urging his horse into a slow walk. "One third of the way there."

"But we're already on the fourth day," Newt said

grimly. "Where does the map say we should go next?"

Even the horses seemed to look at Gerard, who pulled the map out of its packet and unrolled it. He stared at it for a long moment, then looked up at them.

"It's not glowing anywhere."

SEVEN

They finally settled on heading east by the simple expedient of Newt tossing his dagger, a handspan of sharpened metal with a horn handle, into the map and determining that they would head toward wherever it landed. When Ailis withdrew the dagger, she ran her fingers over the narrow hole, frowning slightly. And she gasped when a spark jumped off the map into her finger, then back down again into the map, sealing the rip behind it.

She looked carefully at the map, rolled it up, and handed it back to Gerard. She mounted her mare and turned her in the right direction, waiting until Gerard was ready before touching heels to flanks and starting on their way.

They hadn't traveled more than an hour when Ailis asked, "Is it glowing yet?"

"Not yet."

Farms gave way to scrub woods, and then the trees grew taller and thicker around.

"Is it glowing yet?" Newt asked this time.

"Not yet."

"We're going the wrong direction," Newt said in disgust.

Ailis took offense at his words. "There's no guarantee that the other direction was right, either."

"Yes, and the next talisman might be in Eire, kept by the wee fairy folk, for all we know!"

"It might be in Avalon," Ailis added, finally pushed to annoyance by all Newt's whining about how terrible magic was. "It might be in Palestine waiting for us to find the Grail and trade for it! It could be anywhere, so why wouldn't it be where the map sends us? We have to go on faith. That's what it's all about. Faith. Trust. Belief."

"Gullibility." Newt spat the word like it was a curse.

"Why are you so miserable?" Ailis demanded. "Why can't you—"

"Why can't you leave me be? I'm not your slave to order around and—"

"Children . . ." Gerard rode between the two of

them, interrupting the bickering before they could get worked up into a decent lather. "Ailis is right. We have to trust Merlin. If finding the talismans were impossible, he wouldn't have sent us on this journey."

"You really believe that?" Newt asked.

Gerard stared straight ahead between his horse's ears, watching the way the shadows flickered off the leaves from the setting sun behind them.

"I have to," he said finally. "I have to believe. Otherwise we might as well go home. Besides, Merlin proved himself before we were even born. He helped bring Arthur to the throne. That's more than we can say."

"Who gets to say when we have proven ourselves?" Ailis asked, keeping the same even tone of voice with obvious effort. "At what point have we done enough? Will returning triumphant with the talismans be enough? Or will they pat us each on the head and send us back to our chores?"

Gerard flinched as though the words physically hurt him. He had obviously wondered the same thing more than once.

"Let's worry about getting home and waking everyone up," Newt said, making his own sort of peace offering. "Then you can argue over what sort of reward you deserve."

"I'm not looking for a reward," Gerard said.

"Of course you are," Ailis said acerbically, glad for a more familiar target. "It may not be phrased as such, but you want to be rewarded, the same as we do."

"I just want—"

"To get attention. To be recognized. To be treated as an adult, not a child."

"All right. Yes." Gerard glared at her. "Are you happy now?"

"It's not about being happy. It's about—"

"Glowing."

"What?"

"The map's glowing!" Newt pointed at Gerard's saddlebag, which was, in fact, emitting a distinct blue light through the leather.

"Excellent!" Gerard reined in his horse and turned in the saddle in order to pull at the straps, withdrawing the tube. Blue light ran up and down his hands to the wrist, flickering like a living thing.

"What does the map say?"

"Hold on!" His horse stopped, confused by the strange shifts of its rider, and the others pulled in alongside him. He unrolled it with one hand, tucking the tube under his other arm.

"We're on the right track."

"What is it doing?" Ailis moved her mare closer, looking over Gerard's arm to see what the flickering light was showing. "Oh."

A thin blue line, the color of the deepest summer sky, ran along the road they were traveling on, running farther into the distance. As she watched, it pulsed, beginning at one end and running all the way down the inked road.

"So, we keep going?"

"We keep going." Gerard studied the map, squinting a little to make out the markings. "I think the line ends at this town. I can't make out the name, but it's the only one between here and there, so . . ."

"So let's go!" Ailis said, her voice rising in excitement. "Come on, I'll race you!"

She dug her heels into the mare's sides, slapped the reins, and took off down the road.

Gerard and Newt looked at each other, their eyes meeting in perfect, uncomplicated agreement, for once.

"We *cannot* let her win," Newt said, and kicked his gelding into a gallop, leaving Gerard lagging behind for half a second before, with a whoop, he was racing forward as well.

* * *

"Next time, steal her a slower horse," Gerard told Newt, staring sourly at Ailis, who was trotting gaily several lengths ahead of them, laughing in delight at having won their impromptu race. There was a creek in the near distance with an arched wooden bridge rising over it. Beyond that lay the village that was their goal.

"I didn't steal it."

"You took it without permission." Gerard was trying to be annoyed about losing, but the sheer joy of the race had left them all in an impossibly good mood, despite their situation and the weight of fear that still rested on their shoulders.

"It's not stealing if you're taking it for payment. We didn't get dinner or the promised sleeping quarters, so the mare was payment instead," Newt claimed.

"A mare isn't the same payment as a meal."

"Merlin would back me up."

Gerard snorted. "Now you're using the enchanter as support for your position? Considering your stance on magic, that's not too convincing. Besides, Merlin's as mad as those villagers, in his own way. I'll tell you one thing—Sir Lancelot wouldn't agree with your logic."

Newt shrugged, not disagreeing with either of Gerard's statements about the two men. "Lance is a good man. Too good, maybe."

The squire frowned at that comment. "How can you be too good a man?"

"Sometimes you need to be bad in order to get things done properly."

"That makes no sense at all." Gerard shook his head. "Good is good and bad . . . isn't. It's that simple."

"Nothing's that simple, squire. Not in the real world."

"You know so much about the real world, stuck in the straw mucking out horses? Don't make me laugh." He kicked his horse, rode up to join Ailis, and left Newt fuming behind them.

"What was that all about?" Ailis asked, turning around in her saddle to look at Newt, who had slowed his horse even more, the better to sulk privately.

"He's a fool."

"So you've said before." Her voice clearly said that she didn't agree with him. Rather than argue, Gerard took out the map and studied it again.

Shaking her head, Ailis nudged her mare forward. "Oh, what a pretty bridge," she cried. "Look at the stonework—it's prettier even than the stonework on the walls in Camelot!"

"Pay to pass."

The horses started at the sudden, booming voice. Ailis and Gerard both had to haul hard on the reins in order to keep their animals from bolting when a huge form pulled itself over the bridge's railing and dropped—surprisingly lightly for its bulk—on its feet in front of them.

"Pay to pass," the creature insisted. It was as wide across as it was tall, a block of grayish-white skin covering bulky muscles. Black tufts of hair stuck out from its misshapen head and ears, and its mouth was designed more for tearing than speaking, with a row of jagged teeth that made Gerard think that bolting might be a good idea.

"A bridge troll!" Ailis was delighted. "I've only ever heard of them—I didn't know there were any left!"

Gerard had a sudden thought that his companion was passing insane.

"What do we do?" he asked uneasily. Ailis might be unhinged with her fascination for things like this, but at least she knew what it was and what it might want.

"Pay it, of course. They're usually satisfied with something you're fond of—it's the act of paying that's important, not how expensive it is. Don't you know *anything?*"

"I know how to fight. How to negotiate with honor. How to read and do figures. I don't know how to bargain with creatures that shouldn't exist."

Ailis sighed in exasperation. Gerard was being mulish again, his chin and mouth set in lines she knew far too well. Sometimes, only sometimes, she agreed with Newt's opinion that Gerard really did take himself far too seriously.

Ailis reached into her pocket and pulled out a small wooden carving of a swan in flight. She held it in her hand for a moment, feeling the smooth texture, reliving the memory of her father giving it to her just days before his death. She had carried it with her ever since. She then held it out to the troll, making sure to hold it flat on her palm so that the troll could see it clearly.

"Here," she said, brushing aside a sharp pang of grief. "For my passage, something dear to me."

The troll stepped forward, making the horses shy

even more, and sniffed once as it lifted the swan with surprising delicacy, considering how gnarled its hands were and how long the claws that curved from its fingertips.

"What about me?" Gerard asked out of the side of his mouth when the troll turned its small, shiny red eyes to him expectantly.

"What about you?" Ailis asked, her tone of voice clearly wondering at his obtuseness. "Pay your own crossing. You must have *something* you can offer!"

Gerard stared at the troll, who stared back at him with unblinking eyes. Finally Gerard sighed and dropped his hand to his saddle and untied a thick braided cord from a ring on the leather.

"Here." He handed it over with obvious reluctance, and the troll snatched it from him as though afraid it would be withdrawn if it didn't act fast enough. From the expression on Gerard's face, the troll wasn't wrong.

"Paid." The creature sounded almost regretful, even as it clutched its new treasures. "Pass."

"Let's go," Ailis urged him. "I don't know how long those things will hold him."

Gerard didn't need to be told twice. The horses' hooves made an odd echoing noise as they clattered on the stone archway, making Gerard look down nervously, afraid that the structure would give way. But the footing remained solid and they were over and back on firm ground within moments.

"What did you give it?" Ailis asked, turning back in the saddle to look at the bridge one last time. The troll had disappeared completely and the road behind them was empty. She frowned for a moment, thinking that there was something she had forgotten, then shrugged and turned back to her companion.

"Nothing important."

"It had to be to you, for the troll to have accepted it. Come on, tell me."

"It was a favor, all right?"

"A favor?" Ailis almost giggled but caught herself in time. Favors were given to knights when they set out, from the lady they were paying court to—or who wanted them to pay court to them. "Who was it from?"

"I'm not going to tell you." Gerard's cheeks had turned bright red and he refused to look at her.

"All right." She would find out eventually, once they were home. Camelot kept no secrets from her. "So what is the name of this village, anyway?"

"I don't know, I couldn't read it last time." He

was clearly glad for the change of topic, but uncomfortable that he couldn't answer her.

"Oh, here, let me." She put out her hand imperiously, expecting him to hand the map over without hesitation. Gerard was bemused to discover that, when she behaved that way, he was ready to do as she commanded.

Only he looked down as he was handing it over to her and almost dropped the precious object into the dirt.

"It's stopped glowing!"

"What?"

"It's stopped—" He shut his mouth and handed her the map. Let her see with her own eyes, then.

"Why did it do that? Is there some kind of magic here that's fighting it, maybe?" He hadn't thought of that, being more concerned that they had gone in the wrong direction somehow, or that the magic had worn off.

"I hope not," he said. "We never even wondered if whoever cast the sleep spell might be watching to see if anyone left the castle, if they know that we rode out and—"

"You think they've found us?" Ailis's eyes got even wider and her face took such a pinched look that he was sorry he had said anything.

"No." And he didn't. He might not have Ailis's instinct for magic, but he trusted his own intuition that there was no one on their trail. He glanced at the map again. "Do you think Merlin's magic has worn off?"

"No," Ailis said. "Even if he is trapped in an ice house, I think Merlin's too powerful for that. Magic's a strange thing," she went on. "I mean, not that I know much about it, but I've listened. Merlin once said that you had to have the magic inside you—be born with it, I suppose—to even start learning how to use it properly. But lots of things have the magic inside them. Like that troll. It's magic—it knows when something's worth the toll, like your token. And it casts its own sort of spells. It makes you forget it's there after a while, so it doesn't get chased away. It even makes you forget if there was anyone behi— Oh no! Newt!"

The troll's spell broken by her words, the two of them turned their horses and raced back to the bridge. But Newt was nowhere to be seen.

*   *   *

The squire had ridden ahead in a snit, Ailis with him, which was fine with Newt. Let the two of them go ahead together. He needed some time alone anyway. Much of his days had been spent alone; there were others around, but they didn't speak to him, and he didn't speak to them, preferring the company of the horses instead, and the dogs before them. Animals made so much more sense. They either liked you or they didn't, but they were honest about it. None of the game-playing and currying favor and spreading gossip that seemed to occupy so much time in court.

Ailis and Gerard made so much of Camelot, as though it were the greatest—the only—place in all England to live. It was just a place. Quality animals, decent food. But it was just a place. You didn't get too attached to any one place.

Newt clattered onto the stone bridge, slowing his gelding down enough to look out over the side. There was barely enough water to earn the title of creek, but he could see from the banks where flooding had cut through. He suspected that after heavy rains, the knee-deep trickle might become dangerous.

Then something below shifted, the noise catching his attention.

"Hello?"

A shadow floated on the water and, reacting

instinctively, Newt slipped off the horse's back and onto his own feet. If something wanted to fight, he was going to be where he knew *how* to fight. Leave tossing each other off horseback for the knights.

There was a heavy thud behind him, then: "Pay to pass."

Newt, like Gerard, had never heard of a bridge troll. But he knew that anything that demanded payment in that tone of voice was not something he wanted to deal with. You might pass unhurt . . . or you might not. Arthur could talk all he wanted about might not making right, but the king wasn't here, and a creature that looked dangerous *was*.

Backing up and turning around slowly, Newt felt the cool stone of the railing against his back. Putting one hand behind him for balance, he lifted himself over the rail slowly, letting the beast's attention remain focused on the gelding. Newt would regret losing the animal, but not so much as he would regret losing himself.

And if the creature intended no real harm, then no harm would be done. . . .

Still holding to the railing, Newt dropped over the side of the bridge. His arms straining, he hung there before seeing the ledge underneath where the creature had doubtless been hiding, waiting for unwary travelers. It was a disgusting mess, like the worst kind of magpie's nest, filled with straw and bits of cloth and small shiny objects.

"Ugh. That smells disgusting." But something in the midden caught his attention, and he dropped lightly to his feet onto the ledge, intending to reach for it.

"Pay to pass!" that voice insisted again.

Newt heard the sound of his horse's hooves breaking into a full gallop as it fled across the bridge. Then he felt something heavy hit him between the shoulder blades, and he knew nothing more.

*   *   *

"How much trouble could he have gotten into so quickly?" Ailis wondered out loud as they started back toward the bridge. Gerard just looked at her. He'd only known the stable boy for a few days and already he knew that was a foolish question. Newt's inability to be respectful of authority was a disaster waiting to happen, even before you began considering his attitude toward magic—which would include, no doubt, a bridge troll.

"You know he'd refuse to pay. Let's only hope the troll hasn't eaten him."

"Oh, a troll wouldn't do that!" Ailis said. But they were both thinking of the sharp teeth and the long claws, and neither of them were entirely certain what a bridge troll *might* do if a passerby did not have anything suitable to pay with . . . or if the troll happened to be feeling more hungry than greedy.

They had tied their horses to a tree far enough from the bridge so as not to attract the troll's attention, and stashed their packs under a particularly thickly branched stickerbush to keep them safe from a passing thief. Gerard kept his sword with him. It was the first time Ailis had ever seen him actually wearing it, rather than carrying it on his saddle. She wasn't sure if it made him look brave or foolish, perhaps both.

She wished she had some kind of weapon as well.

"Do we call him, or . . . ?"

"Is the troll going to ask us for another payment? Because that cord was the only thing of value that I had, other than this sword, and the only way that troll's taking that from me is if I leave it thrust through its chest. Just so we're clear on that."

"I don't know," Ailis admitted. "Only one way to find out." She took a deep breath, then shouted "Newt! Are you here?"

The only sounds were the shiishhhing of the water below the bridge, and birds in the trees to either side.

"No Newt."

"No troll, either," Ailis pointed out.

"Unless it's busy—"

"Ugh." Ailis glared at him. "Don't even *think* that."

"Well, he's not here. . . ."

"Underneath of course," Ailis said suddenly. "Trolls live *under* bridges."

"Oh. Of course," Gerard muttered as Ailis started walking again, still cautiously, not toward the stone walkway that spanned the water but down the muddy banks to the left-hand side. Then, suddenly realizing that he was about to let a girl walk, unprotected, into possible danger, he followed, moving quickly enough to catch up with her. He might not like the stable boy overmuch, but Newt was a companion on this quest, and they would not abandon him.

"Watch out for the troll."

"Tell me something I don't know," Gerard muttered back. They both ducked to look under the bridge and gagged at the smell that hit their noses.

"Oh, disgusting." Gerard flinched, holding his forearm against his face, as though that would protect him. There was an alcove under the bridge made of the same stone, running the full length and half the width of the bridge. It was filled with debris, the source of the smell. Water rushed just a handspan below, doing nothing to clean the air.

"There!" Ailis cried, pointing. In the far corner— in the darkest corner of the alcove—something moved.

"Careful!" Gerard held back. "It might be the troll," he said as Ailis splashed through the water and climbed onto the ledge. She turned her head aside slightly as the smell intensified.

"Help me!" she cried softly over her shoulder. "It's Newt!"

Gerard took a deep breath, trying to suck as much air into his lungs as he could, and then waded into the stream to follow her.

"He's been tied up and gagged," she told him, "and seems to be out cold. Let me . . . we have to move him before the troll comes back."

She grabbed Newt by the ankles, trying to pull his bound form out of the alcove. It must have woken him because he suddenly flailed wildly, trying to kick out at his attacker.

"Newt!" she whispered loudly. "It's us! You're safe!"

Either he heard her or he just ran out of energy, because his body went limp. She was able to move him a little bit, dragging him on the stone. He moaned so low that she could barely hear it. "I'm sorry," she said, still tugging. "Gerard! Help me!"

Gerard reached in and grabbed just below her hands, lending his strength in one hard pull that dragged both Newt and Ailis out of the alcove. She squeaked, Gerard stumbled, and all three of them landed in the stream, two of them soaked to the waist in cold water, Newt flat on his back in the current. The cold water started him struggling again. Gerard reached down and slung Newt over his shoulder, slogging to the bank of the stream and, leaving Ailis to follow on her own, looking around nervously for the troll.

"What happened?" she demanded, once Gerard had cut the badly tied ropes off his legs and arms and pulled the wad of dirty rags out of Newt's mouth. He dry-spat once, moved his mouth, and made a face at the taste, then shook his head slowly. "Something jumped me."

"Why didn't you just pay the toll? We were able to pass without any problem."

"Not going to pay anything. It's not the king's toll."

"You should have just paid," Ailis said.

"Easier than getting trussed up for a troll's dinner," Gerard agreed.

Newt snorted off the lecture. "But then I wouldn't have found it," he said, sounding smug, or as smug as a near-troll-dinner could be.

"Found . . . it?"

"Found it," he said, rolling over on his side and opening up his jerkin to show a glass vial identical to the first talisman, nestled safely inside. "Be glad you dropped me on my back," he said grimly.

"Luck again. This much luck makes me nervous," Gerard said, taking the talisman and holding it up to the light.

"What *is* it?" Ailis said.

"Two halves of . . . something." Gerard turned it upside down, then sideways, trying to puzzle out what it might be.

"Does it have to *be* something? Can't they just . . . be magical?" Newt looked at Ailis, who looked at Gerard, who looked back and shrugged. "I have no idea. It's exactly the same as the first one. . . ."

"Troll!" Newt was on his feet, pointing at the

creek. Gerard tossed the talisman to Ailis, who caught it and backed up the bank, looking behind her for a place to hide it and herself. The troll had returned, and from the look on its hideous face, it wasn't happy to see its captive escaping. It raised its arms over its head and let out a gurgling scream as it rushed into the water at them.

Gerard sloshed forward through the water, drawing his sword and getting into a defensive posture. The troll didn't even seem to notice the blade as it lunged at Gerard, who met the charge directly. The muscles he had built during his training with Sir Bors and the other squires absorbed the shock, and his leather jerkin deflected the worst of the troll's claws. But the sheer size of the troll knocked him onto his back and he hit the water with a hard splash. His sword was knocked from his hands and slipped, blade first, into the muddy water. As he fell, Gerard reached up and wrapped his arms around the troll's body and pulled the creature into the water with him.

All Newt could see was furious splashing and thrashing, troll skin, and the now-sodden brown of Gerard's clothing occasionally coming into view.

"Help him!" Ailis screamed from the opposite bank.

"How?" he yelled back. "I can't even tell—"

The two figures rolled, and Newt had to move quickly to get out of the way or get knocked down himself. Nice of the squire to offer himself up as first victim, but it didn't look like he was doing much, other than getting a thrashing before they all got eaten.

Brawn wasn't going to do it; the two of them together wouldn't be able to take on that thing.

Newt looked around for Gerard's sword, but couldn't find it in the churning water. Reaching down to where his own blade should have been, Newt found only an empty sheath.

"No!" Then he waded furiously back to the ledge where the troll had stashed him, frantically searching among the trash for the dagger. Please, let it just have fallen out. . . . A sharp sting on the palm of his left hand told him he had found it, or something suitably sharp. He shifted his hand and closed his fingers around the bone hilt of his blade.

Barely a hand's-length long, the dagger was useful for cutting tangled reins, skinning rabbits, and gutting fish. He doubted it was going to do anything on troll hide. But he felt better having it in his hand. The squire was starting to rub off on him.

"We're still going to die," he said. Then he pivoted

and returned to the stream, where Gerard had gotten his head and shoulders above the waterline. He was now on his knees and wrestling with the troll.

"Yeaaagghhh!" Newt shouted, throwing himself onto a thrashing gray-white arm and slashing at it, trying to not cut Gerard by accident. If he could only distract the creature, Gerard could find his sword and . . .

A heavy arm knocked Newt in the head and he staggered, shaking the water out of his eyes. A salty liquid dripped into his mouth and he wiped the blood off his forehead with his free hand.

"Newt! Do something!" Ailis cried again.

"I'm trying," he muttered, then circled around and made another jab at the troll from behind. The troll roared, its head turning to watch this new threat. Newt moved his blade, the sunlight catching against the metal and reflecting into the troll's eyes.

"Come on, come on!" Newt taunted it, then swallowed hard when the troll let go of Gerard with one hand and reached wildly for him. Newt splashed backward, trying to keep out of reach without getting so far away that the troll would go back to Gerard.

On the bank of the stream, Ailis shoved the

talisman under the nearest bush, then looked around wildly for something she could use to help in the fight. "Something. Anything."

Grunts and muffled swears came from the water. Ailis wanted to hit something, she was so frustrated. She didn't know anything about fighting, not really—just what one of the older servant girls had told her to do if a man ever tried to get too friendly when she didn't want it. She didn't think that would work on a troll. Her gaze suddenly fell on the side of the bridge where some of the stones had fallen out onto the ground.

Before she could talk herself out of it, Ailis scrambled down the muddy bank and sorted through the stones, trying to find one with the right weight and shape. She ended up with two possibilities. Leaving one within easy reach at her feet, Ailis picked the other up in both hands, then judged the distance between herself and the three figures in the water.

"Don't think," she told herself. "Line up the shot and then do it." *Don't think.* She took a deep breath, judged the distance again, and then shifted the stone into one hand and put all of her strength into the throw.

There was an odd whistling noise and the troll

staggered. Through the water in his ears, Gerard thought he heard Ailis whooping. With the part of his brain that could still think, he wondered what she was doing still there, why she hadn't run already. *Get the talisman out of here,* he thought at her, as though she could hear him. *We're not important, the talisman is!* Then the troll pressed its burly, scaled arm against his throat, and even that bit of thought fled. Lacking anything else to do in retaliation, Gerard craned his neck forward and bit the nearest available troll-flesh hard.

Newt heard Ailis's scream of victory. But there was no time to look and see what she had done—the troll was off balance; if he didn't take advantage of it, they'd be taking Gerard back to Camelot on a funeral bier.

Crouching as best he could in the hip-deep water, Newt slid and twisted somehow, drawing on every rough-and-tumble fight he'd ever had—not only with other boys but with the hounds he had cared for as well. And as he slid and twisted, his arm moved almost independently, the hand holding the dagger stabbing upward, not to where the troll's stomach was now but where it was going to be by the time Newt finished moving.

He felt the blade make contact with the troll's upper thigh, slicing into the skin with only minimal resistance. The troll let out another horrible yell, like something was stuck and dying in its throat, and tried to swipe at Newt, who was still moving and already out of reach.

The stagger and the distraction were enough for Gerard, however, to escape the troll's chokehold and flip the creature onto its back. His muscles straining under his wet jerkin, Gerard did his best to hold the beast under the water, trying to drown it. Newt came back around, pulled the blade from the troll's leg and shoved it, point first, into the fleshy skin under the creature's rock-hard chin and rucked it around until he was rewarded with a steady spurting of thick troll blood.

"Is it dead?" Newt asked, gasping. A sudden surge in the troll's body answered him. Newt added his strength to Gerard's, trying to keep the creature's head underwater. Then suddenly Ailis was splashing to their side, throwing herself onto the troll's torso to keep it in place, so they could focus all their attention on the head.

The blood-spurt slowed, then stopped, the thick blood pooling before the current began to move it away.

"Oh, God. I hurt." Newt dropped to his knees

momentarily, then got to his feet and shook himself like a horse whose saddle had just been taken off. He offered his hand down to Gerard. "Come on."

It seemed to take an enormous amount of energy to simply reach up and take the offered hand, but Gerard finally managed it. The other boy's hand was slick with blood and sweat, but reassuringly human.

Legs shaky, the two half-supported each other to the bank, Ailis trailing a step behind. Each of them was trying to wrap their minds around what they had just done.

The feel of stable ground under his feet was almost alien, and Gerard stumbled as he climbed out onto the bank. He thought briefly about looking for his sword, then decided that he needed to rest first. He knew a knight should look to his weapons before his body. But he was just so tired.

The three of them sat down heavily on the bank, staring at everything but each other. Even the effort of speaking seemed to be too much to ask.

"My mouth tastes like troll," Gerard said suddenly in disgust.

Ailis, facedown in the grass, let out a muffled snort, and then another, until she was laughing hysterically.

"It wasn't that funny," Gerard said, making faces as he tried to work the taste out of his mouth.

"No, it wasn't," Newt agreed, his eyes almost tearing from holding back his own laughter.

"I hate both of you," Gerard said, looking down at his mud-covered clothing with a rueful expression. The leather cuisses on his thighs were so waterlogged as to be useless except as weights, so he stripped them off and let them fall to the ground with a sodden thunk. The troll floated facedown in the creek, the water around it fading from pink back to clear as the current carried the blood away. With a sigh Gerard got to his feet and waded back into the water.

"What're you doing?" Newt asked.

"My sword," he said as though it should have been obvious.

"More to your left, I think," Newt said. Gerard shot him a look that clearly said "and I should trust you, why?" but moved slightly to his left. A minute later, his searching hands came up with his sword, wet but undamaged. He slogged to the side of the creek and handed the sword, pommel-first, to Ailis, who found a still-dry corner of her skirt to wipe the worst of the moisture off it. Gerard hesitated, then went back into the water.

"What are you doing now?" Newt asked, still lying on his side on the grass.

"Not going to let this thing foul the water," Gerard said, tugging the troll's body to the opposite bank and pulling it onto the grass. Then he waded back in to splash as much of the mud off himself as he could. "Ugh."

Ailis rolled over onto her back and sat up to watch him. "We could have died," she said finally.

"Yes."

"We almost did die," Newt said.

"You would have died," Ailis said. "If we hadn't come back."

"And you two would have gone on and never found the second talisman," he retorted, a little stung.

"What I mean," Ailis said, "is that any one of us—even two of us—wouldn't have managed it. That's all."

"Point taken," Gerard said, sloshing up onto the bank and trying to wring out his shirt. "So what?"

"Nothing. Just . . . thinking about it, that's all."

The three of them lay there silently thinking about it. Then Gerard stood up again. "Well, while you think, I'm going to get a change of clothing."

"There's the mark of the castle-folk," Newt said, taking his own boots off and shaking the water out. He wriggled his toes in the grass. "They have two sets of clothing."

"Whereas the stable-folk live in the same shirt, year in and year out. And wash it once a year whether it needs it or not," Gerard retorted.

The bickering was familiar, but the tone was too weak to have any real venom.

Gerard went up the bank and down the road to reclaim the horses, muttering something about ungrateful servants who wanted to be troll-food. Ailis stretched her arms overhead, fingers pointing toward the sky, and tried not to look at the bloated body of the troll across the stream, or think about her swan stashed somewhere in the troll's lair or—ugh—on it's body.

"Why can't the two of you just get along?"

Newt shrugged. "Because he talks more than he knows. And because it's fun."

Ailis looked heavenward, as though searching for help in understanding the male mind, then collapsed back onto the grass with a sigh.

None of them wanted to stay near the troll corpse any longer, so as soon as Gerard returned wearing dry clothing and leading the two horses, they decided to move on.

"Do you have any idea what happened to your horse?"

Newt stood up and brushed himself off, then put two fingers into his mouth and let out an astonishingly piercing whistle. Gerard's horse snorted and shifted, while Ailis's stood placidly. Newt waited a few seconds and then whistled again.

"I guess it wasn't as well-trained as you thought?" Gerard started to say, when the sound of faint hoofbeats on the road came to them and Newt's gelding appeared. The saddle was slightly askew, and the horse's eyes were a little wild, but it otherwise looked unharmed.

"Good horse," Ailis praised it. "Good . . ." she looked at Newt expectantly. "What's his name?"

Newt looked blank. "Horse?" There had never been a need for it; he was the human and the horse was the horse, and that was that.

"Loyal," she decided.

"That's a good name," Gerard said, surprising everyone.

"Loyal, then," Newt said in a tone of humoring a madwoman. He adjusted the saddle and made sure the girth was tight around Loyal's belly, then tied his boots by their laces and hung them around his horse's neck and swung, barefoot, into the saddle.

"So?" He looked down at the two of them. Ailis looked at her own shoes drying on the grass, and did the same as Newt, grimacing at the way the saddle felt against her wet clothing.

Gerard had already forced his feet back into his boots and mounted easily. Now he unrolled the map. It was glowing again.

"North," Gerard said, tracing a finger along the path of the glow. "We go north."

More confident in the map now, they started across the field, bypassing the town entirely, riding at a slow, steady trot. They had two of the three talismans, yes, but time was quickly running out. Midnight would mark the end of this fourth day of the seven Merlin had said they had. They had to move faster, or risk losing Arthur and his entire court forever.

*　　*　　*

They're doing rather well, don't you think? Merlin was proud, despite himself.

Smart enough, but no smarter. You could have chosen better. Nimue's voice was scornful.

They chose themselves. That's how it goes, if you care to remember.

Such frail reeds. How can they possibly grow into anything to depend on? And they're moving too slowly.

How much faster could they go? He was indignant at the slur on their behalf. *They're children.*

There are no children in this country, she replied. *You've eaten them all up, you and your precious king.*

And Merlin sighed, unable to argue.

*   *   *

They rode for several hours, stopping only to build camp when it became too dark to see the ground in front of them, although the map in Gerard's hands glowed with a faint, insistent blue light, as though trying to push them on.

"Enough," Ailis told the map sternly. Gerard merely stared at it, trying to decide if it was a magical warning of some sort. "We have to sleep. Otherwise we're going to be even more stupid than we were at the bridge, and get ourselves truly killed."

She could have sworn an oath that she heard the map let out a tiny sigh, and the light flicked off.

Gerard's eyes went wide. "How did you . . ."

Ailis shrugged, then walked back to where Newt was building a small fire a few paces away from where they had placed their blankets. She was beginning to forget what a bed felt like.

"I'm too tired to eat," Newt said when she offered him the wrapped-up chicken from the tavern.

"I've never been too tired to eat," Gerard said, coming to sit down next to them. "Give it to me."

"Excuse me? Who sneered when we took it in the first place?"

"Me," Gerard said willingly. "But I'm hungry and you're not, and it's not going to keep much longer, so I might as well eat it."

"Oh, for pity's sake," Ailis said. "The two of you are worse than a pair of cats, forever hissing at each other for no reason other than that you're there. Should I toss cold water on you and make you behave?"

"Already did that," Newt said.

Gerard just grunted and slid his blade from the scabbard that had been stacked with the rest of their belongings. Stepping into a grassy area away from the horses, he slowly began to move through the basic sword forms. Being away from classes was no reason to let himself get rusty.

"Why must you bait him, Newt? You two would get along if you'd only try."

Newt shrugged. "We are what we are. I'm a

servant. You're a servant. He's a squire of royal family. He's going to be a knight. Knights aren't friends with servants. They may spend time with them, talk to them. Quest with them even. But they're not friends. And they're never ever anything more than that, either. We all have our roles to play." He glared at her as though daring her to contradict him.

"I know," Ailis said quietly. "I've always known that. It doesn't matter."

Ailis went to where her pack lay on her blanket, sat down, and brought out a small ivory comb Lady Melisande had given her last Yuletide, that she'd fortunately had on her person when the bandits stole her pack. Unbinding her braid, she drew the comb though her hair, counting softly until she reached one hundred strokes. By then, Gerard had put his sword away and eaten his share of the leftovers. He was now sitting by the fire, quietly discussing with Newt possible answers as to what the talismans might be or do. Ailis listened to each of them repeating the words of the riddle, making no more sense of it than they had when Merlin's magic first etched it into ice. She thought about joining them, but decided that she was too tired to move again. So she lay down and went to sleep, trusting them both to keep her safe during the night.

EIGHT

"Again I ask, why can't magical items be hidden in a cottage next to an apple orchard, half a day's ride from home?" Newt wasn't joking.

"Because if the quest were easy, the prize wouldn't be worth anything," Gerard said. They had the map open between the two of them, looking down at it and then up in the direction it was leading. Up and up. Into the Hills. It had been two days since leaving Daffyd's keep, and their exhaustion was matched only by a growing sense of desperation.

"According to who? That's particularly stupid. Why should the value be on the finding rather than on what the thing itself can do?" Newt was clearly close to losing his temper, reacting less to Gerard's words than his own frustration.

"That's not what I meant. Never mind, I don't

expect you to understand." Gerard didn't know why he said that, except it was easier than trying to explain what it was he meant.

"What's wrong?" Ailis had brought the horses down to a stream to water them after their grazing, taking advantage of the break to stretch her legs. Being on her feet felt odd after so many hours in the saddle, and she wasn't sure if she would ever get the rocking feel of a trotting horse out of her bones, no matter how many leagues she walked.

"The map wants us to go up into the Hills."

Ailis looked down at the map and then up where Newt's finger was pointing. She noticed in passing that he had started biting the tips of his fingers, almost to the point where they were bleeding. He hadn't done that before—this quest was starting to take its toll on all of them.

"And that's bad, going into the Hills?"

"It's not good," Gerard said. "The Pax Britannica's always been shaky there. Arthur's folk are coastal and he's always had support down here, but up in the Hills . . . the tribes there acknowledge Arthur—they don't have any choice—but they don't always listen to him. We've had to go up there a few times to remind them whose law they live under now."

"We?" Newt raised an eyebrow at that.

"We, in the sense of not being Them," Gerard said, and Newt's eyebrow went back down.

"But that's where the map says to go," Ailis said.

"Yes."

"So why are we still here? We have only another day to find the third talisman and get it back to Camelot." She looked at both of them pointedly, then turned her back on them and swung herself onto her mare with an ease she would not have believed five days before.

The Hills weren't actually all that impressive in terms of elevation. But the roads led upward more often, and the neatly planted fields were replaced by rougher swathes of greenery, little of it tended or farmed.

Gerard got jumpier and jumpier the farther they went, until even Newt took pity on him and stopped making comments about how many spearmen could hide behind a specific rock or tree.

"I didn't know it would bother him so much," he said, defending his words quietly to Ailis as they rode alongside each other on the path.

"Yes you did," Ailis said in an equally low tone. "Because you're not a fool. You might have spent your entire life behind keep walls, but he's been trained to go out beyond them and fight just the sort of thing you're teasing him about. Only he hasn't had a chance to do that yet, and now he's out in it and it scares him."

She stopped, not having quite realized the truth of her words before she said them.

"He's scared," she continued, "not of getting hurt. But of not being able to do what he was trained to do. Of not being able to protect us."

"I don't need protection."

She shot him a glance so full of scorn it should have straightened his unruly curly hair. "Like you didn't need help back at the bridge? Don't be an idiot. I've seen death"—the only reference she could make or would ever make to the battle that swept through her home village and that led to her becoming a Queen's Ward—"and I want someone trained in the arts of war between me and my enemy at all times, thank you very much."

"So why are you out here, then?" Newt sounded genuinely interested.

"Because . . ." She fell silent for a moment, then gathered her courage and spoke quickly, as though afraid that her throat would close around her words if she hesitated. "Because I had to be. Because . . . don't tell Gerard. But in the Great Hall, that night . . . I think . . . I thought I heard a voice telling me to go with you."

"A voice? Someone told you? Who?"

Ailis was sorry she had said anything the moment he jumped on her words. "I don't know. It wasn't anyone there. It was . . . a voice in my head." The reaction she got, a dubious glance and a faint but undeniable shifting away of both horse and rider, was exactly why she hadn't mentioned it earlier. Hearing voices in your head was not something to admit to. Not unless you were a saint—and she had no illusions on that matter. God was not speaking to her.

"I thought it was Merlin," she admitted.

"But he didn't say anything when we saw him—"

"I know. I know." It had been eating at her. Not only that she had failed to bring it up, but that the enchanter had been silent.

Newt thought about that for a while as their horses picked their way along the stony trail. "Still. He was sort of distracted. A cold backside can do that to a man, I'm told."

Ailis giggled, as he had intended her to do. He might not be able to protect her from warriors, but at least Newt could distract her from the things inside her own mind.

"Have you tried talking to him? Merlin, I mean."

"How?"

"How did he talk to you?"

"Magic, of course." She waited for his inevitable reaction to the word, but he merely shrugged. "So?"

Ailis blinked at him, her brown eyes wide. "I don't have any magic!"

"I didn't notice him talking to me," Newt pointed out with maddening logic. "And if Merlin had said a word to Gerard, you know that he would have told us. In great steaming detail."

She laughed again and he felt well rewarded, despite the "why can't you be quiet?" glare the squire turned on them from his position several paces ahead of them.

"Gerard." Newt ignored the look Ailis was shooting him and waved the other boy to join them.

"What now?" Gerard looked from one to the other and, sensing the tension, turned to Newt. "What?"

"Tell him," Newt said. "You know we can't keep secrets like that, not from each other."

Reluctantly Ailis repeated what she had told Newt.

"You hear . . . voices." Gerard looked like he didn't know if he should call for a priest or a healer. Or both.

"Not voices. A voice." Ailis didn't want to be talking about this. It was all right to hear it, so long as she didn't think about it. Or talk about it.

"Merlin's voice," Newt said. He was only trying to be helpful, and didn't understand why Ailis scowled at him so.

"I'm not sure," she admitted. "And he's not telling me anything useful."

"Now there's a surprise," Newt said, with a hint of sarcasm, and made an innocent "who, me?" gesture when they both looked sharply at him.

"How long has this been going on?"

Ailis shrugged, resenting Gerard's tone, like he was the lord of them all, just because his father had been raised with the king. She ignored the fact that he was a squire and would one day be a knight, and she and Newt were only and would probably always be only servants . . . just like she'd always known and ignored, hoping that the inevitable distance wouldn't come to pass.

"Ailis, it's important. For how long?"

"A year. Maybe a little more." The first time it had happened she'd been sleeping. The voice had come in a dream, and sounded as surprised as she had felt. After that it spoke only occasionally, usually when she was trying to decide what to do or how to react to something.

"It never . . . whoever it is doesn't give advice, or tell me anything specific. It's just . . . pushing. It pushes me. To do things or not do things, or just stop shivering like a chicken." That was the exact phrase he had used once. It had been apt and humiliating.

"And you think it's Merlin because . . ."

"Because it feels like him." She couldn't put it any better. The feel of him in her mind, the weight of his silent voice *was* Merlin.

"Why you?"

"I don't know!" Did they think she hadn't wondered that, too? Maybe he was speaking to half the people in the castle. Maybe he wasn't even speaking to her at all and she was eavesdropping somehow on another's conversation. Or maybe she was imagining it all, hearing a voice where there was nothing but her own thoughts.

Ailis didn't think so. But how did you know if you were mad or sane and being spoken to by a surly enchanter? And was there any real difference?

"Have you ever, you know . . . talked to him? Not

in your mind, I mean, but actually—in the castle?" Newt asked.

Gerard looked at the other boy as though he were the one who had lost his mind, asking that.

"He's spoken to me," Ailis said. "Not about anything, just . . . casually."

"Casually? Ailis, Merlin doesn't speak to anyone casually." Gerard still remembered his one encounter with the man in the Council Room before this quest began. One face-to-face exchange in all the years he had lived in Camelot, and it still unnerved him to think that the enchanter had known his name; even now, knowing that past and present had collided in the enchanter, he knew of Gerard then because of the now. . . .

Gerard stopped trying to untangle that reality. Nobody understood how Merlin could live backward in time, not even King Arthur. It was enough for mortals to simply accept that he did.

"So why didn't you ask him when—" Gerard stopped. It was a stupid question. An enchanter, already cranky from being trapped in a house made of ice when he should be helping his king, was not the person to ask about conversations he might or might not have been having in a servant girl's head.

"Why are we even talking about this now?" Ailis asked. "If he's able to give us help, then we should take it, not pry apart the hows and whys." She was near tears at what felt like an attack on her, when Gerard held up his hands in surrender, indicating that he wouldn't talk about it again.

Newt watched the two as Gerard tried to back away clumsily, and felt the worm of worry in the back of his head. What if it wasn't Merlin who'd been "pushing" Ailis? What if it was someone less kindly inclined toward them—or their quest? After all, somone with powerful magic had enspelled the court to stop the quest for the Grail. Could he and Gerard trust Ailis in this? Or might she, all unsuspecting, be leading them in the wrong direction? She hadn't actually asked Merlin about his talking to her, after all. Why not?

He hated thinking like that. He wasn't a warleader, or a manor-lord. But the thought, once landed, wouldn't go away.

* * *

Gerard reached forward and stroked the neck of his horse, trying to calm himself by the act. His skin was prickling; he *knew* they were being watched. And the longer they rode up this path, the more certain he was of it. The hills rose to their left, scattered with boulders that could hide half a dozen watchers, all of them ready to fall upon three travelers. Especially when two of the travelers seemed to think that they were on a pleasure ride of the sort the queen organized every spring, to rid her court of their winter quarrels. Except, from what Gerard had seen, more fights broke out then than during the winter, when they were bored, yes, but under Arthur's eye.

Something prickled his hands and Gerard looked down. The map, now sadly creased, though remarkably—magically—unstained, was glowing more intently now. A faint blue light was pulsing against his palm.

He really didn't want to stop here, not now, when there was so much opportunity for an ambush, but he knew he couldn't afford to ignore the map, especially with so little time left. So he compromised, letting the horse have its head just a little bit, trusting that it would keep to the narrow path and not spook at anything unwarranted. Gerard used both hands to unroll the map enough to see what the glow wanted to tell them.

"Damnation." Gerard felt like using stronger words, but his training held. Instead he merely picked up the reins again and waited for the others to catch up with him, still keeping his attention at least halfway on the hillside. "We have to change direction."

"Which way?" For the first time, Newt didn't ask why or how he knew. The maplight had faded back to its usual narrow blue line, but Gerard still remembered its rather insistent directions.

"Up there." He didn't point, but there was only one "up there" it could be. The hills they had been riding in were children to the taller peak casting its shadow over them—not a mountain such as Gerard had heard of, farther west in the wilds of Cymry, but higher than those around Camelot. Higher than any Gerard had been on before, since Sir Rheynold's lands were bounded by fertile soil, not rock; not so easy to defend but rich enough to feed and house the fighters he needed.

Gerard didn't like heights. It was that simple.

"I don't suppose the road turns and leads us . . ." Newt stopped when Gerard shook his head. "Right. I'll wager there's at least one broken leg before this is all through."

"So long as it's not one of the horses'," Gerard returned. It sounded better when he thought it than when he said it somehow. But Newt nodded, understanding. People could be carried. Horses would have to be abandoned or killed if they were unable to travel.

Ailis, who had pulled her horse alongside Gerard's, finally finished her scrutiny of the map and placing the figures on the parchment in relation to where they were. "We're going to have to climb that?" The two boys nodded. "All the way to the top?" Newt looked at Gerard, who shrugged.

"As far as we have to go and no farther," Gerard said. "And stay together. Remember what happened at the bridge."

"I'm not likely to forget," Newt said, wincing.

*   *   *

In the end they led the horses more than they rode, stepping carefully and moving single file through bushes with sharp-edged, gray-green leaves that none of them could recognize, and stepping on carpets of ugly yellow flowers that let off puffs of pale yellow smoke when crushed. The smoke smelled surprisingly good, but none of them had the inclination to investigate further. The landscape was too strange, too unnerving, for them to linger longer than it took to cross it. And the sun was moving across the sky, reminding them of how dangerous it would be to still be climbing on this uncertain ground come sunset. The only saving grace was that the higher they went, the cooler the air became, until even Gerard, with his leather jerkin, was only sweating lightly.

When they stopped for a midday break, Ailis refilled their waterskins from a tiny stream running downhill while Gerard studied the map and Newt checked the horses to make sure that they hadn't picked up any stones in their hooves that might cause trouble later. Those chores accomplished, they each ate a handful of the dried meat strips from the pack and washed it down with the water. Ailis then disappeared behind an almost-wide-enough tree, while the boys did what they needed to do on the other side of where the horses were tied. Oddly enough, they had all become more aware of the need for privacy since their quest began, not less—the boys even more so than Ailis, who was accustomed to sharing a sleeping room and chamber pot with seven other servants.

"How much farther do you think?"

"I don't know. The map isn't glowing as much as it was before, but we're still on the right track." Gerard looked as disgusted as Newt normally did when talking about magic. "I think Merlin enjoys making things impossible."

"No," Ailis disagreed. "I don't think he enjoys it. I just don't think he knows any other way to be."

"That's a comfort."

Ailis giggled. "That's what my Lady Guinevere says as well, when the king tells her that."

"What else do they say about Merlin?" He had never asked her before. Servants might gossip about their betters, but a squire's responsibility was to be quiet and loyal and wait until called upon. But he was serving Arthur and Camelot directly now, to the best of his abilities, and he thought maybe that had earned him absolution from this small sin.

"Oh, that he is insane."

"He is," Newt said, joining the conversation from behind on the path.

"We should all be so mad," Gerard said thoughtfully, remembering his own encounter with the enchanter in context with what he knew now.

"Does he really live backward in time? Is he getting younger as he ages?"

"I think so. Lady Melisande, one of the ladies in waiting, says that when Arthur first took the crown, Merlin's hair was entirely white. But Melisande wasn't there then; she came to Camelot with the queen, so I don't know how true it is."

"They say that Merlin doesn't approve of Sir Lancelot," Newt said, clearly less hesitant about gossiping than Gerard. "Is that true?"

Ailis hesitated for a short time before responding to that. "There are some who say that Merlin was jealous because the king loves Sir Lancelot so well."

"You don't think that's true?" Gerard had heard those rumors before as well.

"Arthur is fond of Lancelot . . . but he *depends* upon Merlin. I think there is a difference. And Merlin is wise enough to know which is more important."

"More important than having the king's personal favor?" Gerard had to chew on that to make it palatable.

"Before Lancelot there was Merlin. If Lancelot falls out of favor, there will still be Merlin," Ailis said.

"And how likely is it that Lance would fall out of favor?" Newt sounded outraged at the thought, although it wasn't clear if it was from the idea of his hero failing or the king being fickle in his affection.

"So long as the queen stays out of it, not likely at all," Gerard replied. He almost bit his own tongue at his indiscretion.

"Gerard!" Ailis was outraged. "How dare you

repeat such, such filth! 'Tis untrue, all of it!"

"All of what?" Newt asked.

"Some say that the queen has an uncommon fondness for Lancelot. And has since he first came to court." Gerard took no pleasure in saying it, but having opened his mouth he felt obliged to continue, if only so that Newt didn't assume something even worse.

"Lance? But—"

"They're fond of each other, yes," Ailis said. "As suits a queen and the king's champion. But no more. The rumors are but evil words thought up out of a winter's boredom."

Further discussion was, to Ailis's relief, cut short by a flash from the map distracting them all from the topic. They began to look about more carefully and soon found themselves on a level, grassy area large enough, Ailis thought, to hold all of the kitchens from Camelot and room to build a bonfire besides.

The only cover consisted of five or six scraggly, stunted trees, their leaves barely budding despite it being well into spring, and lower, green, prickly bushes. Still, the place seemed safe enough for a short break. Newt was willing to live rough, but Ailis and Gerard both preferred to warm the dried beef strips in some water to reduce the strain on their teeth and jaws. Moving branches aside to see if there was any deadfall to use in building the fire, Newt let out a low whistle and gestured for the other two to join him.

Set into the base of the stone face of the cliff, rising perhaps three times a man's full height and wide enough for a wagon to enter with space to spare, was the entrance to a cave. More of the prickly bushes grew around it, obscuring any path that might have led to it, but the smoothness of the stone indicated that it was not a recent or accidental opening.

"In there?" Ailis sounded uncertain, hesitant.

The map pulsed strongly once and then faded entirely.

"I think that was a yes," Newt said.

"Wonderful."

"Afraid of the dark?" Gerard challenged her.

"Not at all. I'm afraid of what might be *in* the dark. The map points us to where the talisman is. But it's not so good on telling us where the danger is. Merlin forgot that bit of help."

"Next time, we'll remember to ask for it specifically."

"Next time?" Ailis's voice rose until she realized that Gerard had, against all experience, made a joke.

"The horses won't like it in there," Newt said. "We should leave them out here. Ailis, you can stay—"

"No," she said. "No. I—" She took a deep breath. "I will be all right. And I don't think we should split up. Bad things happen when we're not all together."

"Only once."

"Once was enough. Ailis is right." Gerard took his sword and the map, and squaring his shoulders almost unconsciously, started walking toward the mouth of the cave.

"Wait a moment!" Newt called. Gerard paused long enough for the other boy to tie the horses' reins loosely to exposed tree roots. That way each horse would have enough room to move and graze, and should danger threaten, they would be able to pull free rather than end up as another creature's lunch.

"All right. Let's do this." Newt pulled the dagger from his belt and held it in one hand as though he were about to attack a meal. With the other hand, he reached out and took Ailis's hand. Her fingers were cold from nerves, and he squeezed them once, gently, as though to say, "Me, too."

Together they walked across the uneven ground to where Gerard waited, and the three of them entered the cave.

NINE

The change from sunlight to darkness was gradual; the light came several paces into the cave before being smothered by the cool darkness. Newt's eyes adjusted first and he took the lead, still holding Ailis's hand.

The walls were smooth to the touch. The three were soon able to see tiny flecks of light reflecting from them.

"There's some sort of crystal in the rock," Gerard said and then stopped, listening to the odd echoes of his voice moving up and down the walls. "This place is big," he said after the echoes died down. "Really big."

"What do you think made this cave?" Ailis asked.

"Magic?" Newt's voice coming out of the darkness seemed somehow detached from the body that was standing next to her and holding her hand. "Everything else we've dealt with has been magic— and where else would you store a magical talisman than in a cave formed by magic?"

"All right, wise man," she responded. "Then *whose* magic made it?"

Ailis felt him shrug. "Haven't any idea."

The cave narrowed as they walked, then split into two huge chambers; one leading to the left, the other to the right.

"What now?" Ailis wondered. "Get out the map, Gerard."

"Shhhh." He waved her down, and only then did she realize that she could see them both as dim shadows in the dark. Either their eyes had adjusted or it was somehow lighter back here. "Do you hear that?"

"No," Newt said quickly. "Let's go the other way."

"Newt!" Ailis was laughing again, even though the noise scared her into a cold sweat, too. It was low, like the sound of waves pulsing at night, and soft, like snow falling, and sharp, like the crackle of dry wood set aflame. And, somehow . . . alive.

"That way," Gerard said without consulting the map.

Ailis wanted to argue—that was the direction the

noise was coming from—but he was right. She could feel it, weirdly, in her bones, like the way she knew it was Merlin when he spoke to her. She reached out and took Gerard's hand in her free one. His palm was sweating but his grasp was firm, and they walked three abreast into the left-hand cavern.

The sound grew even louder, rising and falling with the pounding of their hearts until Ailis began to think that she had been born hearing the noise and would die with it in her ears.

Then the cavern ceiling rose dramatically, and they stopped dead.

"Oh, dear God," Gerard said on a prayerful breath, his voice cracking on the last word. The crystal chips embedded in the walls here glinted even more brightly, picking up the soft golden glow of a treasure hoard piled high and deep on the smooth stone floor. It was larger than anything the three had ever seen before, a kingdom's ransom in precious jewels and metals; coins, swords, armor, even a great silver-chased chair laying on its side and draped with a Romanesque surcoat that shimmered with a faint green light. Newt stared at it, then looked away, his eyes suddenly hard and shadowed.

But all that glittering, glowing treasure was

dwarfed by the creature that lay curled atop the hoard.

"Oooohhhhhhh . . . " That was all Ailis could manage. Her heart, which had stopped on the first sight of the beast, resumed its frantic beating. Even in her panic she could feel a grin of wonder stretching across her face. From the elongated, muscled tail that draped down off the hoard and curled around it on the floor; to the tightly folded wings that hid most of the body; to the thick, arched neck; to the tapered, triangular head that only looked delicate compared to the rest of its body; the beast exuded two distinct messages: magic and extreme danger.

"That's a—" Newt found his voice, only to lose it again.

"Dragon. Yes. I thought they were all dead."

"Our worse luck they're not," Gerard said. They were all speaking in the smallest whispers they could manage, terrified that the beast would wake.

The dragon's silver-blue scales flickered like will-o'-the-wisps, shimmering first here, then there, until it made you dizzy to look at it. The creature's head shifted, and they held their breath, but the great eyes remained closed. The noise they had been hearing was the great beast's snores.

"The talisman's here?" When Gerard nodded

yes, Newt let escape a swear word so pungent that Ailis felt her skin turn pink, and Gerard looked impressed. "Come on, then. Let's get this done with."

They tiptoed around the chamber, trying to spot something in the priceless heap that glowed the same way the first two talismans had.

"There!"

"Where?"

"Up there!"

Newt pointed, and the other two let their gazes follow. One of the dragon's scales up on the side of its head was glowing.

"I'm going to kill Merlin. If we get out of this alive, I swear, I am going to kill him. I don't care if I have to do it as a rat." Newt clenched his hand more tightly around his dagger, well aware that it would be completely useless.

"I'll help you do it," Gerard vowed. Ailis just stared.

"We're supposed to take a scale off a dragon?" Newt continued, almost too angry to be afraid. "Off a *dragon*? Ailis, you talk to Merlin. Do it now. Tell him he's even more insane than I thought before."

"It's not a scale," she said. "It's a ring."

It was. The dragon wore a single golden ring set

into one small, delicate-looking ear which you could only see if you tilted your head and looked at the dragon's face from a certain angle.

"A ring. We're supposed to take a ring off a dragon's ear. And this is easier than getting a scale?"

"It's not," Ailis said petulantly. "Merlin, if you're listening, this is truly not fair!"

"Hmmmmmppphhhhh." A giant exhale of air and sound.

Ailis looked at Newt, who looked at Gerard, who looked at Ailis. And then all three of them looked at the dragon.

One great black eye opened, then another, and a puff of smoke rose from the tremendous nostrils. The dragon was waking up.

"Scatter!" Gerard yelled and all three split up, heading in different directions. The lessons hard-learned under the troll's bridge came into play almost instinctively. Ailis and Newt went left, crossing and recrossing each other's paths, while Gerard jinked to the right, stopping short and starting again, all three keeping an eye on each other, circling and dodging so that one of them was always moving away from the dragon and one was always moving closer.

The dragon raised its head slowly, its neck

arching as it rose so that it had a good view of all three of them. Its eyes operated independently, keeping track of two of the three at any given time. Then the head darted forward, cutting one of them off and forcing them to scramble in another direction, until they were reacting from it rather than distracting it. It was old and canny; as canny as Newt, as smart as Ailis, and as determined as Gerard, and the three humans wore out long before the beast did.

"Stop playing with us!" Gerard roared finally, pulling his sword from its scabbard and racing toward the nest when the dragon's head darted at him one time too many.

Newt and Ailis both changed direction when they heard Gerard's roar. They brought him down to his knees and forcibly dragged him out of the dragon's striking range.

"Are you moonstruck?" Ailis demanded in a loud whisper. "Getting killed won't help anything!"

"Indeed it won't," the dragon said.

The three of them froze. Dragons. Talking.

"This is so unfair," Newt said, dropping Gerard's leg and folding to the floor in a pose of resigned exhaustion. "Why is everything bigger, nastier, and toothier than we are?"

Think, girl. Use that brain I suspect you have somewhere.

"Merlin?"

"He's talking to you again?" Newt tried to take his gaze off the dragon to look at Ailis, but couldn't bring himself to do it. "Tell him I'm going to kill him."

"I don't know. I think . . ." She couldn't take her eyes off the dragon either, watching with fascination as its neck extended, bringing the narrow head closer to them. The dragon's eyes were huge, bottomless black orbs, and the smoke rising from its red-rimmed nostrils smelled, strangely enough, like the kitchen's herb garden back home—sweet and spicy and of greenery and dirt, all mixed in together. Ailis found herself drawn to it, swaying on her feet as the dragon's head moved closer.

And Newt did for her what they had both done for Gerard. He shoved her hard enough to wake her from the trance the dragon's smoke had put her in, enough to make her skip back several steps, out of reach of the creature's sharp-toothed mouth. The dragon was no herbivore, that was clear. And while it couldn't make a meal of her entirely, its mouth was certainly large enough to take an arm or a leg at a time.

Ailis wasn't sure what Merlin had meant about

using her brain, if it was Merlin at all and if she wasn't merely imagining things. She didn't feel all that intelligent right now. Just scared. Still, she knew she had to try.

"Wise One," she said, trying to sound reproach-ful, the way you would speak to a merchant who was offering less than his best goods as a bargaining chip before starting serious discussions. "Wise One, you see before you three who would trade with you."

She had no idea what she might trade for a dragon's earring. But if it worked for the troll, the trick would be to get the beast interested in the idea. They could worry about details later.

"Hmmmmmmmmm." The great eyes closed half-way, scaled lids dropping down in a move that fooled no one into thinking the dragon wasn't paying atten-tion. "Trade? Hmmmmm. What, little human? Why would I do that?"

The voice was deep and dark, sending shivers down Ailis's spine.

"To acquire new treasure without effort." Her voice ended on an upswing, making it sound like a question, and she cursed herself for it.

"I don't mind effort," the dragon said. While its expression didn't change, she could swear the voice was amused now. It was playing with them, just as it had been before. "And yet, you smell different, of places I have not been in many, many years. Perhaps . . . perhaps you have something that might intrigue me. What have you of worth, to tempt me into giving over something of mine?"

Gerard got to his feet slowly, trying not to draw too much of the dragon's attention, and moved just behind Ailis, careful to keep his hand away from his sword's hilt. Newt, already by Ailis's side, rocked back onto his heels but otherwise didn't shift.

"Ah . . ." Ailis thought hard. "We have three horses outside, well-fleshed and grain-fed. Excellent eating." She jabbed Newt with an elbow when he would have protested. "We could bring them to you or let them free for you to hunt, as is your pleasure."

A snort sent a darker, thicker cloud of scented smoke rising into the cavern, and the dragon yawned, showing off two rows of wickedly sharp teeth. "I would be more interested in hunting something that gave me more challenge." The meaning was clear, and Ailis heard her companions swallow hard.

"I'm afraid I cannot offer you . . ." Was it better

to say more or stop there? She decided that less was better, at least until she knew what the dragon was thinking. Was it a serious counteroffer? Or was the dragon planning to eat them *and* the horses no matter what?

Gerard jumped in, his voice surprisingly steady. "You say you have not traveled to where we come from in many years. Few dragons have. Our king would be grateful were you to allow us to take back the item we came for. . . . And the gratitude of a king is no small thing."

"The gratitude of kings is a very small thing. How can one being say a word and bind another to it? Are you this king's own self, to speak for him?"

"I . . . no. But he—"

The smoke rose in a trio of rings from each nostril. Gerard stopped talking.

Newt stirred but didn't say anything. The silence drew out an uncomfortable tension; the dragon, still coiled lazily around its hoard, stared at them with those unnerving eyes.

"Me." Gerard looked as startled as anyone that the word had come from his mouth.

"You?"

"I'm offering me. Not as food," he was quick to

say. "As a . . . servant. How many other dragons, Wise One, no matter what their treasure, could boast a squire—a human servant—of their own?"

"You wear the armor of another; their sigil is on you." The dragon's eyes were terrifyingly sharp, to notice and recognize the design on the left shoulder of Gerard's jerkin: the emblem of Sir Rheynold's house. "You cannot serve when you are already sworn. And I would not desire a servant who cannot stay true to his vows."

The tones of the dragon's voice seemed familiar to Gerard, and he fought to stay focused on what it was saying, rather than trying to chase down that familiarity.

"I have sworn no oaths," Newt said finally, getting to his feet with obvious stiffness.

"Nor I," Ailis said.

The dragon craned its neck to inspect first Ailis, then Newt. "You are not so well-dressed. You are servants already—there is no satisfaction in having servants serve."

"I've been sneered at before," Newt said, his voice shaking with what might have been either fear or laughter, "but never so well with so few words."

That earned him one large smoke ring, blown

directly into his face. Newt coughed, turning away from the heavy, bitter smell.

"I'll make you a vow," Gerard said, stepping forward until he was well within the dragon's reach. "Now I am a squire, and sworn to my master's service. But soon I will be named a knight, and my only obligations will be to my own word. If you give us freely what we came here for and allow us to leave unmolested, when that day comes, I will return."

"And serve me?"

"And challenge you. Fair combat, winner takes all. That will leave us both the subject of legends that will live on forever." He was taking a gamble—the dragon was not interested in objects, or meals, and was too proud to take servants as such. Pride. That Gerard knew something about.

"Are you insane?" Ailis asked in a harsh whisper, her hand clearly itching to slap Gerard for his foolishness.

He merely shrugged, watching the dragon examining them. "Without the ring we might as well die now, because if we can't wake Arthur, the entire country is doomed. Besides," and Gerard actually smiled, although his face was white with tension, "why are you assuming he'd win?"

There was really nothing Ailis or Newt could say to that. So instead the three humans waited while the dragon blew more of its smoke into the chamber, the very end of its tail twitching against the floor of the cave.

"A worthy trade, perhaps. Hmmmmmm. A worthy trade. What is it you would take in exchange?"

"A small thing, a very small thing," Gerard said. "The ring you wear in your ear. That is all."

Ailis would have groaned at the way Gerard tried to bargain, making it clear that what they wanted was no small thing at all, but it had been his offer that was accepted, so he had the right to do it as he would. She only hoped he wouldn't make the dragon rethink the deal and ask for more.

"A ring?" The dragon pulled its head back as though affronted . . . or surprised. The black eyes rolled backward in contemplation. "A ring. Hmmmmm. Hmmmmmm. Yes, yes, I remember. I took it from a pirate."

The tone of the dragon's voice, fondly remembering the incident, suggested that the pirate had not given it willingly.

"And now you want it . . . why?"

"We asked no reasons of you, Wise One," Ailis said firmly. "Reasons cost extra."

The head tilted, and a puff of smoke came out in a dragon-laugh. "So. Take it, human. Come to me and take it."

In the end, it was Newt who stepped forward as the great neck snaked down, lowering the head to within touching distance of the short human. He calmed his heartbeat, calling on everything he had ever learned dealing with injured dogs and spooked horses. The dragon might be wiser, smarter, more fierce, but the trick was still to show no fear; to do nothing that might provoke a regrettable instinctive reaction.

Unlike what he would do with a dog or horse, however, Newt dared not stroke the skin to calm the beast, no matter how inviting the scaled hide might be with its sparkle and sheen. Close up the smell was stronger than was comfortable, a stink of cloying smoke and the sweat of a meat-eater too long without water. He wondered, briefly, if dragons bathed, or perhaps rolled in the dirt to cleanse themselves; and if the wings, unfolded, were like those of bats or birds. . . .

"The ring, human," the dragon reminded him,

the voice close enough to his ear to make him start and perspire.

"Yes. Turn this way, please?"

The dragon obliged, one eye watching Newt's every move, and Newt was glad that his dagger was sheathed and out of reach so he wouldn't be tempted to do anything stupid. In such a short time he'd trusted his life first to an unproven squire, and then to a girl who might be led astray by magical voices, and now to a dragon that could eat him in two bites.

Smiling slightly at the insanity of it all, Newt lifted one hand, letting the dragon see every movement clearly. One finger touched the ring gently. It seemed to shimmer with blue light, calling him to place it on his own finger and carry it away.

"I'm going to unhook it now," Newt told the dragon, hearing his voice crack in the same manner he had teased Gerard about not long ago. "It may tug a little. Please don't bite me if it does."

"I shall not," the dragon assured him gravely.

Contrary to his expectations, the dragon's skin was warm and soft, so much like the delicate flesh of a horse's muzzle that Newt almost let himself relax into it. But he remembered himself in time before taking such a liberty, instead procuring the ring in a delicate pinch and releasing the catch with his other hand.

The ring came away in his hand without any difficulty, and Newt stepped away from the dragon's head with undignified haste.

"You have what you came for," the dragon said, keeping its head low and watching them. "Go now. Bother me no more."

"Once more, Wise One," Gerard said, inclining his head to the dragon, as close as he could manage to the way knights saluted each other on the jousting field. "Once more."

"Indeed. I shall look forward to it, human. I shall be here when you return."

And with that, the dragon curled its head back onto the treasure-heap, closed its eyes, and began to snore once again.

The three humans, the talisman safely captured on Newt's finger, turned and fled the cavern.

More time had passed than they had been aware of while they spoke to the dragon. Night had fallen and the sky was spread out before them, black silk scattered with brilliant stars. The air was cool and crisp, smelling faintly of what they could now identify as dragon-breath—or perhaps the smell came with them, clinging to their clothes and hair.

From their vantage point high up on the hill, the world seemed as distant as the sky.

"You have the talisman?" Gerard asked Newt. The stable boy nodded, unclenching his fingers and displaying the thick golden band on one finger.

"It seemed smaller, somehow, in the dragon's ear," Newt said.

"Do you realize how that sounds?" Ailis asked. "Speaking of a dragon so casually."

"No stranger than speaking of a troll. Or an enchanter in a mystical house of ice. I begin to wonder if my horse will start to speak next. Or the very walls of Camelot."

"They had best not," Gerard said, clearly not happy with the idea that walls might begin to speak.

"At this moment," Newt said, still staring down at the ring, "I begin to think anything at all is possible." He let out a whoop, startling himself as much as his companions and the horses tethered nearby. "Dragons! I took a ring off a dragon!"

"It seems more . . . appropriate a talisman, than the other two," Ailis said. "But do you really think you should be wearing it? It's magical, after all."

Newt blanched, and slid the ring off his finger quickly. He handed it to Ailis without hesitation when she extended her own hand for it, grinning at how quickly he moved once reminded of its origins.

She rested the ring in her palm, tilting her hand first left then right, looking for something out of the ordinary. But the blue magic had faded the moment they identified it, same as with the other two talismans, and it did nothing but glint like ordinary gold in the starlight.

"What do you think they do?" Gerard wondered.

"Do talismans all have to do something?" Newt asked. "Isn't it enough that they just . . . I don't know . . . *are?*"

The two young men both turned and looked at Ailis. She looked up at them and gave a startled little shrug. "I don't know. Maybe . . . wait." She closed her fingers around the ring. "Gerard, get the other two talismans."

He started to question, then thought better of it and went to fetch them from the saddlebags.

"It's stupid of us to have left them out here where anyone might have stolen them," Newt said.

"There wasn't anyone here to steal anything," Ailis pointed out. "The nearest town is hours away. And who would come near a dragon's lair if they need not?"

"Perhaps someone who didn't know a dragon was here? How often do you think he leaves that cavern, anyway?"

Gerard came back with the two glass talismans before she could answer. "Here. What do you think—"

"A moment," she demanded, sitting comfortably on the ground and placing the ring on the dirt in front of her. She reached up for the two other talismans. "Something about that riddle Merlin gave us . . ."

"The talismans had to be reclaimed by 'three who are one,'" Newt said. He looked at the other two doubtfully. "Is that us?"

"I suppose." Gerard sounded only a little reluctant to admit such a thing. "But who's the one who is none?"

"I don't know," Ailis said impatiently. "Maybe Merlin? He was supposed to have been a foundling, not knowing who his parents were. But what I meant was that line about 'one into three.'" Ailis placed the glass objects next to each other, considering them. Wide base. Narrow end. Ends and base each the same distance across, perfectly matching. The narrow end . . . She picked up the ring and measured it against the end of the glass on the left. The narrow end was the same distance across as the inside of the ring. She set it firmly against the end. It stayed put.

"You think . . ."

"Maybe."

She lifted the other glass and turned it upside down, matching narrow end to narrow end, with the golden ring between.

A blast of dark blue light momentarily blinded them, outshining the stars and making the night seem far darker when it faded.

"What was that?" Gerard exclaimed.

"Magic, I'd wager," Newt said in an even tone, his earlier exuberance drained from him. "Isn't it always?" He touched her face gently, making her look at him. "Ailis, are you all right?"

"I'm fine," she said, her voice faint and distant. "Look!"

The three talismans were fused by magic into one piece. Inside the topmost glass, sparkling blue particles of sand appeared, suspended in the act of sliding into the bottom glass, as though caught in time.

But what had caught Ailis's attention was the red flame slowly etching words on the glass the same way Merlin's had given them the original riddle, etched into the walls of the ice house.

Tempus signa proferrit.
Tempus non insisit.
Rex et serva aeque morientur.
Lacrima sola una separet
Lacrima sola una liberaret.
Tempus medicus.
Tempus interfector.
Tempus flumen hic nunquam comprimit.
Incipat. Finiat. Renovet. Renovet.

"We did it," Gerard said, barely able to breathe around the knot in his chest. "The three talismans into one. We did it."

"We haven't done it yet," Newt said. "The riddle said 'three who are one . . . before the moment turns at home.' So for all we know, Camelot's still asleep. Besides, these new words—can you read them?" The other two shook their heads. "Neither can I. And we don't have time to find someone who does. Tomorrow at midnight we're out of time."

"We have to trust Merlin," Ailis said.

"What we have to do," Gerard said, "is make it back to Camelot in time. Let's go!"

TEN

They rode all through that night and most of the next morning, pushing their horses cruelly out of necessity, and trusting the faint blue glow of the map to guide them. It was just before noon when Camelot came into sight. From a distance, the castle looked the same as it ever did. Set on an incline, the castle walls were manned by guards moving slowly back and forth, and the banner that indicated the king was in residence flew on the far watchtower.

But something seemed off. It wasn't until they came closer, almost to the base of the hill, that they realized what it was.

The gates were closed. And the guards were too slight to be full-grown men, despite their armor.

"It's what we feared," Ailis murmured. In the back of their minds, all three had half-hoped that somehow someone—some adult—would have come in and solved the crisis without them. That's the way the world was meant to work, not left resting on their unready shoulders. But Fate had not been so kind, and they were still needed.

"Hurry," Gerard said, and they kicked their exhausted horses into one final gallop.

"Open!" he called as they came within hailing distance. "Open in the king's name! It is Gerard of Abmont and his companions," he added, in case the young guards didn't recognize them.

There was a hesitation. All three of them began to sweat. Then the sound of chains being pulled came through and the great doors began to swing open.

The moment they slipped through the half-open doors, they were surrounded by dozens of children, all of them reaching out, trying to touch the three, grabbing at their clothing, calling their names.

"Silence!" Newt bellowed, and a shocked silence fell on the courtyard, broken only by an anonymous sniffle from a youngster in the crowd.

"Is this how you keep order?" Gerard asked, his voice carrying in the silence. "Is this how you hold Camelot in our absence?"

"Bossiness has always been a problem with him,

hasn't it?" Newt said to Ailis from behind one hand. She bit the side of her cheek to keep from laughing. It wasn't really that funny, but they were so very tired.

Gerard swung down off his horse, wincing as he did so. Even for a squire, riding through the night and past dawn took its toll on the body.

Someone took the reins of his horse and led the beast away for a well-deserved rubdown and treat. Without having to turn around, Gerard could feel his companions dismount and fall in behind him, their presence surprisingly comforting; as much or even more than the three-in-one talisman in the saddlebag now slung over his shoulder.

They made their way through the silent castle to the Great Hall, but Arthur and his court no longer sat at the feasting tables. The Great Hall had been scrubbed spotless. The long trestle tables which had been brought out for the feast were removed, so that only the high table remained. The great salt dish and heavy gold candlesticks suggested that at any moment servants would begin setting the table for the midday meal.

"We thought it best to keep things as . . . normal as we could," Thomas said, meeting them at the door. The squire looked as though, unlike the adult inhabitants of the castle, he had not slept in days.

Gerard didn't care; he only had one thing on his mind right now. "The king?"

"Come with me."

They walked through the castle hallways, unnerved by the soft echoes of their feet on the floor. Thomas didn't seem to notice. Perhaps, after a while, it started to feel normal, the same way the constant noise had been normal, before.

Ailis thought she might from now on always divide her life into Before and After.

"You know how to wake them up?" Thomas asked anxiously.

"Yes."

"We think so." Ailis qualified Gerard's claim.

"You think?" Thomas's voice broke on the last word, making Gerard realize suddenly that his hadn't cracked in more than a day. Or was it two? He wasn't sure. He knew exactly how many days had passed since they set out, but the details of what had occurred were beginning to blur.

"Yes." This time Gerard tried to sound more confident, but honesty compelled him to add, "We have to do it before midnight, though."

They found themselves outside the great wooden door of the Room. Gerard looked up, remembering the last time he had snuck in to sit at the Round Table, to pretend that he was a great knight home from a perilous quest.

He had thought it would feel wonderful, satisfying.

Mostly, it felt tired.

"They're in there," Thomas said with a gesture of his hand. But he made no move to enter the Room.

"All right." Gerard turned to enter the Council Room, then stopped and clapped his fellow squire on the shoulder. "Thank you," he said. "You've done well."

It should have felt odd or silly to say that to Thomas. Thomas should have taken offense, being spoken to that way by someone his own age. But he merely nodded, looked relieved, and stepped back.

"Let's do this," Newt said, stepping forward to open the servant's door as though he had gone through it a hundred times before. Ailis and Gerard looked at each other, both amused by Newt's matter-of-fact confidence.

"He was a dragon in another life," Gerard said, only half-joking, and followed the stable boy into the Council Room.

Ailis proceeded, only to step on Gerard's heels. The two boys had stopped just inside the door.

Arthur sat in his chair, upright, his hands flat on the table in front of him, the bare blade of Excalibur on the table under his fingers. His eyes were closed, as though he had somehow, impossibly, dozed off while hearing the advice of his knights.

Around him, each in his chair, the chosen knights of Arthur's council sat. Lancelot was to his right, Sir Kay directly across the table, Sir Owain and Sir Balin and Sir Marhaus in various poses of interest. Gerard shook his head slightly. Despite the situation, someone had clearly retained a sense of humor when they arranged their masters in their chairs.

"What are you staring at?" she asked.

"They're so . . . still." Newt's voice was hushed.

"What did you expect?"

"I don't know. Are you sure they're still breathing?"

"They are. Just . . . slowly," Thomas said.

The three turned, startled. Thomas had come in behind them after all. He, too, was staring at the Table, but it didn't seem as though he was seeing the knights at all.

"We check on them every day. Make sure they're still sleeping. Dust them occasionally." He smiled at

Gerard weakly. "We took the king out on the walls, yesterday. In case anyone was watching—anyone unfriendly. It took four of us to move him, to make it look as though he was walking on his own.

"Whatever you're going to do," he said losing his poor smile. "Do it. Now. We saw riders outside last night. We thought it was you, but they rode away."

"You think—" Ailis started, then stopped.

Thomas looked at Ailis as though only now realizing that she was there. "I don't want to think. I want my king awake to think."

Newt made a rude noise at that, and Ailis jabbed him in the side with her elbow. Now was not the time to antagonize anyone. Even if he was a fool.

And where were the rest of the squires, anyway, she wondered. Were they all on the walls, guarding?

Gerard took the talisman out of the saddlebag and walked toward the table, something drawing him to the area behind Arthur's chair. Newt went to his left, Ailis to his right. Thomas watched, but stayed where he was. Gerard held the talisman out in front of him, and the other two each placed a hand on the glass, carefully not touching where the letters still glowed.

"Ready?"

"No," Ailis said. Newt merely shook his head.

"Right."

They each had studied the spell briefly, but it had been more important to get home than to learn the pronunciation of those foreign words. Besides, none of them had been willing to risk speaking the spell out loud, before it was time. They just had to trust Merlin. Again.

Tempus medicus.
Tempus interfector.
Tempus flumen hic nunquam comprimit.
Incipat. Finiat. Renovet. Renovet.

They finished, stumbling over the last unfamiliar words, and held their breath, keeping almost as still as the sleeping knights. Gerard raised the talisman, watching the sparkling blue sands.

But the grains remained frozen. Arthur and his knights did not wake.

"Oh, well done, children. Well done. And yet . . . you have failed."

The three spun around at the voice, almost dropping the talisman in their shock. Newt managed to grab it, only a handspan from the floor.

A woman stood in front of them. She was tall

and elegant, her dark hair caught up in a single long braid, with regal features that looked somehow familiar but almost overpowered by huge dark eyes that seemed to see through them, judging them and finding them amusing.

"You've been so entertaining," the woman went on. "I was almost hoping that you would succeed, you've done so well until now."

"You!" Ailis couldn't keep the accusation out of her voice. "Of course it was you. Who else."

"Who is she?" Gerard's outburst clearly confused Newt, who looked to Ailis for an answer.

"Morgain," she whispered. "The king's half-sister. Very wicked."

"Wicked is in the end result, some would say," Morgain said lightly. "My brother might be considered wicked, for all the women he has made into widows, all the children left orphans, all the old ways struck down and his new laws placed over them.

"You have to understand what it is you do, my children," she went on. "That is a lesson Merlin never let Arthur learn. The sin will not continue another generation. Until you understand, I shall not shed a tear for my poor, foolish brother."

A thick mist of dark green descended from

nowhere. When it faded an instant later, Morgain was gone.

"She's the one who did this? Why?" Newt asked.

"Long story," Ailis said. "And most of it I don't know. There's gossip, but nothing they speak about in front of us. The one time Lady Morgain came to court, I remember that it ended badly. She threatened Arthur and almost came to blows with Merlin. Merlin swore that he'd kill her, only Arthur wouldn't let him."

"She's an enchanter as well . . . ? Of course she is," Newt answered himself. "She cast the spell. But why?"

"I don't know," Ailis said again. "Only that she hates Arthur. Horribly."

"And she could not bear to think that Arthur might gain more glory or add to his reputation by claiming the Grail," Gerard added in a grim tone. "But there's a way to end the spell. She said as much. That we *almost* succeeded. We still have the rest of this day. We have to find out how to end it!"

"She was taunting us, Gerard! All of this . . . if Morgain was the one who cast this spell, then there's no hope. Only Merlin can stand against her—Merlin and Arthur—and she's managed to take Arthur down—"

"Ailis!" Newt's harsh exclamation stopped her, making her realize that she was beginning to shout as well. She drew in a deep, pained breath, then let it go and nodded. "Yes. There's always hope. Merlin's guided us so far." She only hoped he could do so again.

"'Understand what it is you do. . . .'" Gerard looked at the talisman in Newt's hand. He reached out to turn it so that the glass ends were vertical. It somehow seemed right that way. "We have to understand what the spell is!"

"But how?" Newt was being the practical one again. "We don't even know what language it's in!"

"Merlin's study," Ailis said. "He sent us to this. It must be a language that he knows."

"Must?" Newt asked, clearly dubious.

Gerard and Thomas were already out the door. Ailis gave Newt a one-shouldered shrug and rubbed exhaustion out of her eyes. "If we don't believe, we have nothing. Haven't *you* realized *that* already?"

"Even if you do believe, you still mostly have nothing. Haven't you learned that already?"

Ailis looked at him with pity. "Trust, Newt. For once in your life, just *trust*."

And with that, she walked out the door, leaving Newt alone in a room filled with motionless sleeping knights.

"Do you understand females any better, your

highness?" he asked Arthur. The silent reply seemed to mock him.

*　　*　　*

"Don't bother with those," Ailis said, scowling at an ebony box filled with writing quills. "They're not magical at all."

"How do you know that?" Thomas had gathered half a dozen helpers along the way, and they all crowded into the rooms that were set aside for the enchanter. The young ones gaped and gawped at the strange instruments and manuscripts scattered everywhere.

"Because . . . I know." She wasn't sure how she knew, but whatever it was they needed, she was confident it was in here. It was like knowing the color of her own hair, or how her feet would move one in front of the other.

A young page reached for a crystal bowl. "Don't touch that!" Ailis snapped, then whirled on Thomas. "Why did you bring them all in here? They're going to break something, or worse, set off a spell accidentally."

That made some step back with more fear than curiosity.

"Ailis." Gerard tried to be reasonable. "We need all the help we can get. They'll follow orders. They won't touch anything we don't give them. Right?"

All but Thomas nodded their heads in agreement. The squire folded his arms over his chest and watched Gerard until his fellow squire lifted one eyebrow and repeated: "Right?"

"Command me, great one," Thomas said then. Ailis, not trusting herself to speak, handed him a particularly heavy book she didn't think had anything worthwhile in it. In the meantime, Newt had placed the talisman on a small round table that he had dragged into the middle of the room so that everyone could see the lettering.

"Look for anything that looks like that," Ailis said, pointing to it. "The lettering or the shape. But don't read any of it out loud!"

She handed out parchments and bound papers she thought might be useful, suppressing a wince when she had to hand them to children younger than herself. None of them should be doing this. *She* shouldn't be doing this. But they had no choice.

Closing her eyes, Ailis let herself sense the room. She reached out for the same feeling she'd had when the voice that might have been Merlin spoke to her, the same sense that surrounded the talismans and the map.

"We don't have much time," Gerard said,

coming to stand next to her.

"I know. I think . . . there." She opened her eyes and walked across the room to a glass-fronted case. Astonishingly it was unlocked. Or it unlocked itself for her—she wasn't sure which would be more disturbing. But she reached inside and took out three small books, each barely the size of her hand and no wider than her thumb.

"Try this," she said, handing one to Gerard and looking around for Newt with the other. "Newt!" He was standing by the door watching the children squinting at the written words and trying to compare them to the words on the talisman. When she called he looked up, and the fear she saw in his eyes cut her suddenly, like a knife so sharp you didn't feel it going into the skin.

"We're going to need more candles," she said. He nodded and beckoned to one of the younger helpers.

Ailis took the two remaining books, found a space on the floor that wasn't already occupied, and opened the first book. The author's handwriting was terrible, and it took all her concentration to decipher it.

Newt returned at some point with more candles, then disappeared again and came back with two kitchen workers carrying platters of food larger than they were. The meats and breads were consumed almost absently, the sound of parchment scraping against parchment interrupted only by shifting bodies and the occasional indrawn breath of hope dashed by a sigh of disappointment until a page named Bets let out a squeal of discovery.

"What is it?" Gerard asked, hurrying through the crowded room to kneel by the page's side. "What did you find?"

"I don't know. I mean, I think it's . . ." The boy was incoherent in his excitement. "I was looking at this sheet of parchment—it was blank—and then I looked at some foreign words on another parchment, and then I looked again at the first one, and there were words there. It looked like what I'd just been looking at, only I could read it. Only now this page is empty again!"

"Easy, Bets. We believe you." Gerard gave the boy an encouraging squeeze on his shoulder, then took the blank piece of parchment away from him and brought it over to where Ailis and Newt waited.

Newt looked over the blank page. "That's a translation spell?"

"Possibly. A useful thing. If we can trust it."

"We don't have any choice," Ailis said. Newt just rolled his eyes.

"None of the magic has steered us wrong," Gerard pointed out. "It's only what we've done with it that's not worked."

"I'd argue that," Newt said. "But not right now. Read it."

Gerard held up the blank sheet of parchment, looked at the talisman, and then, after committing the strange words there to certain memory, looked down at the paper.

And the words appeared in common tongue:

Time marches on.
Time cannot stop.
King and maid alike must pass.
Only one tear may set them apart
and only one tear may set them free.
Time is the healer.
Time is the killer.
Time is the river which can never be halted.
Begin. End. Renew. Renew.

"One tear . . . whose tear?" Newt wondered.

The three companions stopped and looked at each other.

Ailis's eyes lit up with certainty. "Morgain's tear!

She said she wouldn't shed a tear . . ."

"But she's gone, disappeared." Newt pointed out the problem and then added, "And how do you get a witch to cry, anyway?"

"She's an enchantress, not a witch."

"What's the difference?" Gerard wondered.

"Power," Ailis said. "And intelligence."

Gerard sighed. "I was afraid that you were going to say that."

"All right, everyone," Newt said, noticing that everyone in the room was watching them. "Go. Shoo. Wait somewhere less dangerous, all of you." The room emptied out while Gerard found another piece of parchment and a stick of charcoal to write down the translation before one of them misremembered a word.

"Rumors will spread," Ailis said, absently running her hand over the surface of Merlin's worktable, careful to avoid touching any of the various vials of powders, liquids, or oils stored there.

"At least it will be good news." Newt wasn't too worried. "They need that. Besides, it's not as though there are that many people to be gossiping. Unless they've learned to do it in their sleep."

"That's Camelot," Gerard said, wiping the charcoal off his fingers, leaving a long smudge on the side of his trousers. "Even in their sleep."

"I know where she's gone," Ailis said suddenly, turning to face the two boys. "Morgain. I know where she's gone to."

"Where?"

"What? How?"

"Before Merlin left. The reason he left, he'd been fighting with Arthur."

"I remember," Gerard said. "Everyone was hiding under the furniture."

"It was in the solar. Arthur had gone there to hide. Merlin hated going in there, I think the ladies unnerve him, all twitter and giggle.

"But this time Merlin followed him—stalked right in on the king's heels. He wanted . . ." Ailis tried to pace as she remembered, but there wasn't enough room to move, even with only the three of them there. She waved her hands in frustration, trying to recall the actual words. "Merlin said he knew where Morgain was. He wanted Arthur to go there and bind her. But Arthur wouldn't. No matter what she'd done, Arthur still thought of her as his sister. Merlin was furious, yelling at the king that he was going to lose his kingdom over stubborn, stupid affection for a woman who deserved none of it.

"I liked the name of the place he said she was," Ailis recalled, thinking hard. "Something about apples . . . that's what it was. Appleton."

"Did Merlin happen to say where it was?" Newt asked.

"I . . .yes. But I can't remember!" She rubbed her face with her fists, frustrated beyond words. "Argh!"

"Wait." Newt had raised his hand to try and comfort Ailis, when he was struck by a thought. "I know how to get there."

"You do? How?" Gerard turned to stare at Newt, as though to say "*You* know?"

"Not Appleton maybe, but the Isle of Apples. You get there . . . by dying."

"That's not helpful."

"No, really," Newt went on. "I remember hearing once that there was a doorway in the tombs down below the chapel. The story I heard was that it led directly to the land of the dead. But then someone else said no, it led to the Isle of Apples. And the storyteller said they were one and the same. That only the dead might be taken there, and only the damned ever returned."

Gerard swallowed hard and looked at Ailis. "Do

you think Appleton and the Isle of Apples are the same place?"

"Could be. And we don't have a better idea." She glanced again at the talisman. The hair which had escaped from her braid during their wild ride back to Camelot fell into her face and stuck to her sweaty skin. "But since we're neither dead nor damned, that doorway may not work. And even if it does . . . how do we expect to make Morgain cry? Hold an onion to her face?"

"We need to find her," Gerard said, his tone brooking no doubts. "We'll worry about her crying later."

*   *   *

"Dead people make me nervous."

"Don't be foolish, Newt. They're dead. They can't hurt you."

"We have a castle full of ensorcelled people above us, we spent the past six days following a magical map around the land, and we're about to try and go through a magical gateway to confront a wicked enchanter who also happens to be the king's sister, and you're telling me that I'm foolish to worry about dead people? Pardon me if I don't take your word for that, Mistress Magic-Is-Interesting."

The crypt was cool and dark, the only light

coming from the candles they carried. An even dozen of the squires had wanted to go with them, but the others had dropped back when Ailis, listening to the small still voice inside her, told them that only the three who had started the quest could finish it. She might have been wrong, but after everything else that had happened, she was learning to trust that voice, no matter who it came from.

Besides, as Gerard had pointed out, they needed everyone at the ready to secure the castle, just in case the riders spotted the night before returned with reinforcements.

"Dead people." Newt muttered, the candle in his hand shaking slightly as they went down the stairs. "Dead people should be buried or burned and be done with."

The first few chambers were empty. They had just come to the first occupied niche, the king's mother, forever silent in a stone coffin with her likeness carved upon it.

"We shouldn't be here."

"She will forgive us. From the stories I've heard, she was a woman who understood doing what needed to be done."

And then they were at the doorway Newt had told

them about. It couldn't be anything else: a stone archway the height of two men and wide enough across for
all three of them to enter at once. The stone was carved
with figures doing things Ailis didn't dare to identify.
One look at them made her feel slightly queasy.

"Human sacrifice," Gerard pointed out helpfully.
"Sir Bors says it used to be quite popular in some of
the older—"

"Don't want to know," Ailis said hastily.

"So we just go through?" Newt asked.

"I guess so." She refrained from pointing out that
he was the one who had known about this doorway
in the first place.

"I really wish we knew something for certain,
just once."

"I'm pretty certain that simply standing here will
not do anything," Gerard pointed out.

"I hate you." Ailis wasn't sure if she was talking
to Gerard, Newt, or what lay beyond the doorway.

Without further hesitation or discussion, the
three of them extinguished their candles, clasped one
another's hands, and stepped through the doorway.

ELEVEN

Once years ago, Newt had gotten horribly drunk on a wineskin of mead someone had left in the stable. He and another friend had hidden it, denied all knowledge of it when the rider came back looking, and snuck out late at night to drink it.

The dizzy, spinning, nauseated feeling that came the morning after had been the worst experience of his entire life. Until now.

Dropping. Fast, prolonged dropping. They were being picked up by a gust of wind and tossed back up, then down again, spinning as they went. Newt couldn't feel his body beyond the dizzy urge to throw up, but he was pretty sure he was covered in bruises. He felt as though he were being kicked by the largest, meanest battle horse in the stable and then stomped on again for good measure.

When the wind stopped, he could feel his body again. Just in time for it to land, facedown, on something very hard and cold. Then something softer and warmer but very heavy landed on top of him.

"Gehoff!"

There was a grunt, and the weight rolled off him. It had been Gerard, from the clink of the scabbard against the stone below them.

Stone. No wind. They had to be beyond the doorway and at their destination. Newt got to his feet as swiftly as his aching muscles would allow and looked around, squinting in the dim sunlight. They were in a courtyard of some sort; a mosaic of pale golds and deep greens and blues under their feet depicted strange sea-creatures. In the distance he heard the echo of waves crashing against a shoreline. Overhead, the sky which had been pale blue and cloudless when they woke that morning had clouded over so thickly that the sunlight could barely work its way through. And yet, somehow, it did not seem overcast or dark—the light was spreading in such a way as to allow no shadows anywhere.

"The Isle of Apples. Are we dead?" he wondered aloud.

"I don't feel dead," Ailis said.

"How would you know?"

"All right, I wouldn't. But I don't feel dead." Ailis's braid had been pulled loose by the magical winds. She had a nasty bruise forming on one side of her face but seemed otherwise unharmed. Newt did a quick inventory of his own body and decided that nothing was broken; he was only sore. Gerard was already pacing the courtyard, one hand on his sword's grip, the other touching the high stone walls as though expecting to discover a door hidden from his sight.

There were no doors. No windows. No portals. Nothing save featureless gray stone walls rising high above their heads, and the mosaic on the floor that was becoming more and more disturbing by the moment—Newt noticed that several of the sea-creatures were in the process of eating humans.

"I think we've arrived," Ailis said.

"Yes, but where? And how do we get from here to where we need to be?" Gerard asked Ailis.

Brains, child! You were given brains! Use them!

It wasn't a voice in her head this time. Or, rather, not a *new* voice, but a memory of Merlin, particularly irate at one thing or another, storming down the hall-way. He had seen her walking in the other direction and trying so hard not to be noticed. He snapped the words at her, as though she had personally displeased him by some act of notable stupidity.

Perhaps she had. Only not then. Now. How did he keep it all straight? The answer was that he didn't, of course. That's why he was so short-tempered.

"If the doorway led us to this place . . . then this courtyard must open to something. This is merely the entrance hall—the chamber where unexpected visitors might be judged friend or foe, and actions taken accordingly."

"We're not exactly friends," Newt pointed out.

"No. But—"

Gerard came back, interrupting her. "There's a door here."

A door of the sort none of the three had ever seen before, not wood or hammered metal sheet but stones that, when slowly slid aside, revealed an entrance wide enough for them to enter one at a time.

"It may be a trap."

"Of course it's a trap." Ailis sounded as though she had finally lost patience with the lot of them. "You have any other ideas?"

Gerard shrugged and stepped forward.

Passing through this doorway was not as painful

as the other. They left the courtyard behind and entered a huge room, slightly smaller than the Great Hall in Camelot but more ornate, with rich rugs underfoot, jewel-toned tapestries on the walls, and a gentle golden glow coming from hundreds of candles set in crystal holders that reflected their light up and out, brilliant enough to make the stars weep in shame.

And at the far end of the room, seated in a great golden chair shaped like a swan, was Morgain. Her long black hair was loose, falling in a glossy curtain down over her shoulder and pooling in her lap. A great black cat lay at her feet, its green eyes blinking at the three strangers without any curiosity at all.

"Welcome, my dears." Her voice was soft, amused. Her face was a flawless mask.

"To your lair?" Gerard asked.

"To my home." She spread her arms, indicating her surroundings. "Is it not lovely?"

Gerard took a long, careful look around. "It is indeed. All sparkly and doubtless sticky, like a spiderweb. Did you let us in merely to kill us, or did you plan to bore us to death first?"

"Gerard!" Ailis was horrified, astonished, and not a little afraid, but Newt put a calming hand on her arm, pulling her back slightly. He was smiling faintly, as though he had finally figured out what Gerard was doing.

Morgain, rather than being offended, merely laughed. A wonderful laugh, full and rich, and all three were reminded once again that she was Arthur's half-sister. Arthur had a laugh like that. "You have learned your lessons well, young man. Irritate your opponent, insult her. Make her lose control of her temper so that she does something without thought, something to show her weakness. Although it would not be 'her' would it? Always 'him.' Always the man as the opponent." Her good humor had turned to bitterness.

"You are a worthy opponent," Gerard said. "I would treat you no differently than any man."

She looked at him, tilting her head slightly as though weighing the truth of his words. "Perhaps you would. If so, there may yet be hope for my brother's otherwise worthless court."

"A court which you've spelled to sleep," he retorted.

"Ah. Yes. There is that. Is that what you're here about?"

"We translated the spell."

"And do you understand it? Do you truly?"

"Yes."

"Are you certain of that? Without someone to tell you, how can you be sure?" Her eyes sparkled with an evil sense of amusement, and her red-tinted lips curved in an unpleasant smile. Gerard was reminded of an adder hissing its defiance.

"We're certain," Ailis said, stepping forward when Gerard hesitated. Morgain took one look at her, and the smile softened the smallest bit, but was no less predatory.

"Girl-child. How did I miss you before?"

Ailis gulped, but stood her ground. "We understand the spell. 'Time marches on. / Time cannot stop. / King and maid alike must pass. / Only one tear may set them apart / and only one tear may set them free.' Time moves forward for everyone . . . but a tear sets them apart. A tear was used to stop time. And only a tear—likely from the same source—can set time to moving once again." Ailis looked at Morgain as directly as she could. "You cast the spell. I don't think that you would allow anyone else to take part in it. You want this to be personal. Completely personal. So the tear came from you."

"And you think to take a tear from me to end the

spell?" Morgain laughed again, but softer this time. "Clever. Quite clever. I gave you too much of a clue. But, as I said, it is good to know there are at least some in Camelot who can think beyond the way things have always been done." She leaned forward, placing her pointed chin into the cup of her hand and raised one arched eyebrow. "So, tell me. How do you plan to take this tear from me?"

"I thought I would do it the traditional way," Gerard said casually, drawing his sword from its scabbard. "Beat it from you." He was bluffing. Despite his words about treating her as any other opponent, he didn't think he could fight a woman. On the other hand, she was a danger to his king. He would do whatever it took to free his king. That was what a knight did.

Morgain laughed a third time, clearly astonished. "You would challenge me? To battle?"

"Are you afraid to meet the least of your brother's court?"

"Steel to steel? How . . . quaint." She could take all three of them down with her magic. All four of them in the room knew that—five in the room, since it was so obvious even the cat at her feet must know. But there was a point of honor involved. Morgain spoke of not being treated as an equal; she had been bitter when speaking of men's ways. So now she would have to face him using one of those ways. If she could defeat him, she would be vindicated. Justified. Triumphant twice over.

And, as the daughter of Gorlois, a royal daughter of Cornwall with generations of warriors in her blood-line, she had training in the art of the sword. Years ago, before she relied so much on her magic. . . .

"Unless, of course, you are afraid of my skills," Gerard finished.

That did it, as he had known it would. She rose from her swan-throne and strode toward them. As she walked, her embroidered robes changed into a leather jerkin over cloth shirt and pants similar to what the three of them wore, only of much finer fabric. In her hand she now carried a strange blade. The grip was of red wood, and the quillion was a simple black disk that seemed barely enough to pro-tect a man's knuckles, much less an entire hand. She pulled it from a black scabbard and Gerard had to admire the glittering beauty that was revealed. Barely an arm's length and too narrow to be taken seriously, the metal shone like the moon, its oddly shaped tip and tapered edges covered in some strange tracings, like the embroidery on Merlin's robes. Gerard took it—and her—seriously.

She dropped the scabbard on the floor and smiled at him, the smile of a confident woman. "Have at it, then, man-child."

Gerard felt his body fall almost instinctively into fighting stance; knees bent to provide stability and speed, shoulders relaxed, holding up his own much less lovely but stronger-looking blade, ready to attack or defend as needed.

They circled each other warily while Ailis and Newt got out of the way. The cat remained by the throne, watching them all with supreme indifference.

Morgain held her blade in one hand, using the other to balance herself. Each studied the way the other moved, looking for a weakness, an opening. Gerard didn't see anything he could exploit, so he went on the offensive, lunging suddenly, without any shift or change in his body that might signal his intentions.

She met his lunge with a perfect parry, turning his heavier, less gracefully forged blade away and attempting to slide in under his own defenses. But he knew the trick to that, and was out of range before the blow could land.

They had, he suspected, the same teachers—or at

least teachers who taught the same style. But that blade, so exotic looking, suggested that she had learned from other masters as well. Gerard would have to be careful.

Before the thought was finished, he felt her behind him, moving more swiftly than he could imagine, the blade scoring across his shoulder blades and almost cutting through the leather that protected him.

He cursed, turning to face her, reluctant respect in his voice.

"Language, child," she said, still smiling. Then she lunged in turn, her blade shimmering in the candlelight. Gerard refused to be distracted and beat it away with a heavy clang of his own blade and forced himself within her fight-circle. Dangerous, so dangerous; with her speed and the lightness of her blade he was at a disadvantage. He could practically hear Sir Bors bellowing at him now about stupidity and getting killed.

But he was there, barely a handspan from her body, and bringing his sword up for a disabling blow. . . .

Suddenly he was on his back, breathless, his hand holding onto his hilt only through instinct, not intent.

She had kicked him! And, he realized, feeling

the bruise forming already, had she been able to stretch her leg out farther, he would have been incapacitated long enough for her to finish him off.

Gerard rolled left as Morgain came in for the kill. He got to his feet as she spun around, blade outstretched, her face drawn back in a fierce snarl that would have looked natural on her cat.

"Dirty tricks? I should have expected such from you." In fact, he should have. Sir Bors would have had him back at basic trials if he had been there to see such foolishness. Never expect honor from a dishonorable source.

But Sir Bors wasn't here.

Gerard matched her, snarl for snarl, and went on the offensive again. His sword wasn't as nimble as hers, but he knew how to handle it as well as most knights twice his age and experience, and he had an advantage they lacked.

He could play dirty, too.

On his next lunge, Gerard didn't go for any of the usual targets: heart, arms, or legs. Instead, he drove the blade directly at her lovely, unprotected face, aiming for the spot directly between her eyes.

She backtracked, as he'd suspected she would, and tried to regroup. He pressed, moving forward faster than she moved back. It left him slightly winded, but the urgency of the situation gave him stamina he might otherwise have lacked. He beat against her blade once, then again, until she spat at him and leaped out of the way, just before he would have backed her up against a patch of bare wall.

"Never let them get hold of a tapestry, boy," he could hear Sir Bors say. "That's just another weapon you've given them."

He felt the kiss of her blade just as he began to turn, incredulous that she could react that quickly. A small part of his mind dealt with the injury: a shallow slash across the back of his left leg. Bloody, but not deadly. It would hamper his ability to move, however, the longer he had to stand on it. *Finish this,* he thought. *One way or the other, time's wasting. Finish it.*

A flurry of action, lunging and then lunging again, driving her back when she expected to step forward and attack at will. He shut down the part of his mind that was aware of the pain; shut down all awareness of anything save the blades flashing and twisting in front of him, the smell of blood in his nostrils, the feel of the heavy metal in his hand, the *rightness* of it all. None of this was directed; his mind had retreated and let instinct take over in a place that he knew was dangerously familiar to the berserks, the mad warriors of the cold lands Sir Bors told stories about.

But it worked. Without knowing quite how he had done it, he had driven Morgain into a corner, parrying her attack and slamming both blades into the wall, hers held there by the greater length and weight of his.

It could have ended there, but for Morgain's greater speed and agility. Somehow she slipped from that cage, sliding her blade out from under his and spinning almost in his arms to go back on the defensive.

Irate at being bested, Gerard slapped at her, missing her blade entirely and taking a stinging cut on his underarm for it. But the flat side of his blade connected just behind her calves as she turned again, and the blow sent her to her knees, twisting as she fell so that she landed on her backside.

Instinct took over again. Gerard was dark with fury at being cut not once but twice. "Yield," he said, his knee on her stomach, his blade held crosswise against her pale white neck. Up close, she was even more beautiful, her eyes wide and dark enough to fall into. For once, Gerard was almost glad he wasn't full grown. He suspected that, had he been older, those eyes would have disarmed him in a way her sword skills had not been able to.

"I have never yielded," she said through gritted teeth.

"You have never fought me." It was sheer bragging, and Gerard was sorry the moment the words left his mouth—especially in light of the fact that she had, in fact, almost beaten him. Those deep eyes darkened even more, and he felt her shift, even with the blade to her neck. Then he was knocked over sideways by an unexpected assault, and when he recovered from being slid across the floor several lengths he looked up to see Newt and Ailis holding her down, a dagger lying on the carpet between the two of them.

"Poisoned?" he asked, indicating the dagger Morgain had magicked into existence.

"Most likely," Ailis said, breathing heavily. Newt had Gerard's sword and was holding it awkwardly, with the point over Morgain's face, dissuading her from trying anything else.

"Unlike Gerard, I'm very bad with this thing. I might do something . . . clumsy with it. Like rip your face open. That would be a shame, since it's a very pretty face."

"Do it," Ailis said. Her voice was harder than either of the boys had ever heard before. "Kill her." Under the anger, Newt thought he heard fear.

"The king won't like it," Gerard said, coming to stand next to Newt.

"I don't care. Merlin wanted her dead. He doesn't want things without reasons, not reasons we can understand, maybe, but reasons. That is enough for me. Kill her."

"You've been beaten," Gerard said to Morgain. "Your only hope is to use magic again—but Newt will kill you before you can do anything. He has no sense of chivalry. And he will not hesitate to kill a woman, not even the sister of his king." Gerard hoped that was true, anyway. Newt wasn't trained for this. How would he do against a human opponent?

"Or," Ailis said, her fear making her foolhardy, "you might call your servants, of whom I'm sure you have many. But they would see you defeated by three children. And they would never forget that, would they? Their enchanter mistress, the great and terrifying Morgain, brought down by three children, and two of them mere servants."

Morgain moved her head as though to respond to the girl's taunt, and Ailis drew a sharp breath in. "A tear," she said in astonishment.

"A what?" Gerard paused, caught by the urgency in Ailis's voice but not really hearing her.

Ailis pointed at Morgain's neck. Where her shirt had been torn away, something glinted in the candlelight.

With a dubious look at his companion—there was no way she could have seen that from where she was—Gerard placed his hand over Newt's, using the tip of his sword to catch the chain around the sorceress's neck. He lifted it away to reveal a thumbnail-sized gemstone the yellow-red of a new flame.

"This?" Gerard asked Ailis. "A trinket?"

Morgain glared up at him, and he lowered the sword just enough to remind her who had won their battle.

"It's a *tear*," Ailis said, moving closer so that she could see it better. When Morgain turned that glare on her, she stepped back, out of range again. "Look at it! Can't you feel it?"

Gerard looked, shrugged, then winced. All he felt were his muscles telling him how much they wanted to put the sword down and have someone apply a healing poultice to the places Morgain had scored on him during their battle.

"A tear?" Newt asked. He stared at Morgain the way he might a snake about to strike, if you weren't entirely sure if you were out of its range or not.

"A tear!" Ailis said impatiently. "A tree's tear. Amber." On seeing their continued blank looks, she elaborated. "It's magic. I can feel it."

"Witch-child," Morgain said, and her voice was soft again, silky and convincing. "Witch-child, where have they been hiding you in cold, harsh Camelot?"

"I'm not a witch," Ailis said, taking another step away from that voice.

"My tear speaks to you. My magic calls to you. Have they been teaching you, witch-child? Or do they ignore you, pretend you don't exist, save all their power for those born with—"

"I'm not a witch!" Ailis yelled, fear and anger mingling in her voice. "Take it from her, Gerard."

"What?"

"Take it from her! Don't you get it? A *tear*!"

"Oh," both boys said in the same instant, their brains finally catching up with their exhaustion. The spell. A tear. That was what Morgain had used, what they needed to complete the spell's reversal.

"Let me do it," Newt said, when Gerard hesitated, unsure how to take the chain from Morgain's neck without releasing his cold iron sword's hold on her. And Ailis clearly wasn't going to go anywhere near the sorceress.

At Gerard's nod, Newt swallowed hard, then stepped forward and knelt next to Morgain. First a dragon, then a sorceress. He'd been more comfortable with the dragon.

"Forgive me, lady," he said under his breath. "But I am only a stable boy. My place is to serve, not command. And to do so I must take this from you." He didn't really think the polite words would cool Morgain's wrath any, but it certainly wouldn't hurt to try. She merely glared at him as his hands lifted the chain over her head, cupping the amber shape in his palm. He stepped away, out of reach again.

"Run," Gerard said to them. "Go on, get out of here. Take the tear back to Camelot. Hurry!"

"But . . . Gerard . . ." Ailis protested, even as Newt turned to go.

"Do it, Ailis." His voice allowed no refusal, and when Newt reached out to grab her hand, she went with him.

Gerard waited until the other two were clear of the door back into the courtyard, then made a low bow to the enchantress.

"You lost, my lady. Show some honor in this and allow us to return home unharmed."

"Honor? You think I have honor?"

"Yes, my lady." Gerard looked her directly in the eye. "I believe that—despite all I have seen—that you have honor." She was the king's sister, after all.

Morgain stared at him and laughed. Even flat on her back, a metal sword to her throat, she still seemed completely, impossibly in control.

"Go home, young squire. Cherish this victory. It is not the end of the game."

Gerard nodded and, not turning his back on her, walked out of the hall and into the courtyard.

"Why are you still here?" he asked his companions on seeing them standing in front of a wall, the shadowy outline of the doorway revealed if you looked at it sideways rather than directly. Ailis was holding the tear up in front of it by the chain, as though she had been waving it at the walls until the doorway revealed itself. Newt looked torn, as though half wanting to dive through the doorway and half not trusting anything the stone revealed.

"We weren't going without you," Ailis said stoutly. "Idiots! Go!"

Behind them, the sound of a low, long scream echoed, and Ailis turned a shade paler. From beyond the walls around them, Gerard could hear the ocean roar, a thundering sound far beyond any surf or storm he had ever heard before.

"Go!" And he dove forward, arms outstretched to grab each of them, carrying them backward into the half-seen gateway barely a step ahead of the magical storm Morgain had sent to stop them—or, giving her the benefit of the doubt and assuming she would remain true to her given word, to destroy the tear before they could use it.

And then the swirling abyss within the portal swallowed them, just as Gerard felt the first slap of wind-driven water against his leg, and they were gone.

TWELVE

Traveling through magical portals wasn't the most dignified way to travel—or arrive. Gerard shoved Newt off his stomach, and more carefully moved Ailis off his legs. They had been deposited in a tangled heap just inside the doorway on the Camelot side of the crypt.

"Alive?" Newt mumbled.

"Can't hurt this much when you're dead," Ailis said. "I hope, anyway."

"You're back! You're almost out of time! It's nearly midnight!" Finan had clearly been assigned to wait for them. His eyes were wide, like a frightened horse's, and he was practically jumping in place from anxiety.

The three stood and helped each other up. They pushed past Finan on the way out of the crypt and moved as fast as they could up the winding, stone stairs and made their way past the crowd of children that had gathered outside the Council Room.

"Hurry!" Tynan urged them when he met them outside the great door. "I hope to the heavens you have the answer."

"We do," Gerard said, clapping Tynan on one shoulder. He followed Newt and Ailis into the chamber. Gerard faltered for a second as his glance took in Arthur and his knights, eerily motionless in their places at the Round Table. *Please, as God is kind, let this work,* he thought with a sense of desperation.

"Who has the talisman?" Ailis asked.

One of the older pages stepped forward holding out a soft white cloth wrapped around the precious object.

"You know what it is, don't you?" the squire, Dewain, said in awe.

"No, what?"

Dewain shook his head in astonishment. "I saw one once, when my master and I traveled to the Holy Land. It's an hourglass. Sailors use them to keep track of time."

The three of them stared at each other, then at Dewain.

"A timekeeper. I'll laugh about this when we're

done—after I sleep for about a week." Gerard took the talisman and unwrapped it. He and Newt and Ailis positioned themselves the same way they did during the last attempt, each of them with a hand on the hourglass. Ailis opened her free hand to show the tear, still attached to the golden chain.

"Ready?" she asked.

Her companions nodded.

As they spoke the words, by now burned into their memory the same way they were burned into the glass, Ailis very, very carefully held the chain so that the tear balanced on the top of the hourglass.

The amber tear flared a deep red—deeper than blood—and slowly sank into the glass top of the hourglass, leaving the chain still dangling from Ailis's hand. A second of hesitation, and the now-liquid tear slid through the glass, dropping slowly into the frozen sand.

The entire talisman began to glow brightly, dark red and blue swirling around in a pyrotechnic display of magical sparkles. As they spoke the last line of the spell, the sand quivered and began to slowly fall from one glass chamber to the other.

Something in the air shivered. Ailis felt a cold finger slide down her spine.

Well done. Well done, girl-child.

And she wasn't sure if it was Merlin . . . or Morgain.

But Ailis didn't have time to think on it. Without any warning, the knights seated at the Round Table were awake. They were also confused, hungry, and more than a little disoriented.

"Gerard!" Arthur cried as he turned around in his chair and saw his nephew in front of him, exhausted, mud-filthy, and grinning in company with two equally bedraggled children. "*What* have you been up to?"

THIRTEEN

"They're not taking us seriously," Ailis complained. "We saved the entire castle, and every adult in it, and they're not listening to us!"

Ailis and Newt were in the stable—the only place that was currently safe from the renewed flurry of activity within Camelot. It had been two weeks since they woke the castle, and the chaos that followed made a knocked-over anthill seem placid. Everyone had been overworked, trying to repair seven days of missed life. Ailis had finally fled that morning for the relative quiet of horses and horse-boys.

"The king listened."

"And then did nothing," she said bitterly from her perch in the hayloft above him. "He didn't even send anyone out to find Merlin and bring him home! He just laughed and said that Nimue was going to be the death of Merlin, some day."

"Could even a dozen knights have gotten Merlin out of there before Nimue was ready to let him go?" Newt asked.

Ailis didn't have to think about that one. "Probably not . . . no."

"There you go. All's well that ends well, right? Merlin will get himself free eventually, and Arthur's awake and healthy, and the Grail Quest will go on. And here you are, and here I am, both alive and home, and all's well." As he spoke, Newt brought a grooming brush down in one long motion; his other hand rested on the horse's neck, keeping it calm.

"Don't talk to me like you do to Loyal," Ailis retorted. "I'm not that easily placated."

"No?"

She made an exasperated noise, and threw a clod of straw at him. Most of it landed in Newt's hair, which was already dirty with sweat and horsehair.

"I just thought that *something* might change."

"It has." Newt stopped his grooming and looked up at her. "Look at you."

Her old russet skirt and borrowed tunic had been replaced by finer garments—a linen smock and wool kirtle, or loose dress, lightly embroidered at the sleeve and hem. And her ankle-high boots, visible as she swung her legs over the side of the hayloft, were not hand-me-downs, but rather made to suit her foot, from the shoemaker who made footwear for the queen's own ladies in waiting.

"Pffft. Clothing. That's my reward for saving everyone. But what about you? They shouldn't just ignore you like this."

"They haven't," he said, going back to grooming the horse with steady strokes.

"They haven't? That's wonderful! But—"

"But why am I still here?"

Ailis looked around and shrugged. "Yes. Not that this isn't a very nice place, I suppose, but—"

"Because they couldn't offer me anything more than what I already have," Newt said, pausing to rub his nose with the back of one arm before going back to his job.

"Oh, don't you worry about me," he said, seeing her frown with concern. "When I need something, I'll remind them of my service fast enough. And they'll honor it. That's how nobility is. I just don't want anything more right now."

"Still. Somehow it doesn't seem fair."

Newt laughed and Loyal turned his head to look

at him curiously. "It isn't. Life's like that. Speaking of which, have you seen his majesty's nephew lately?"

Ailis looked slightly deflated. "No. Well . . . I have, but only in passing. They're keeping him busy." The Quest for the Grail was still set to go out—late, but intact—and all the squires had been hoping to go, Gerard especially so.

"He's the one who's changed. I told you. I did, didn't I? Knights aren't friends with servants. Not really."

"You're an idiot," a voice came from the stable door. "At least we know that won't ever change."

Gerard was also wearing better clothing than they had ever seen him in. His hair had been ruthlessly trimmed and slicked back, making him seem older, more commanding. But he came in and dropped himself on a bale of hay, careless of his finery.

"I've been trying to find time to come see you both. But they barely let me sleep, everyone's so intent on making this Quest perfect. The things that were done before aren't good enough—the weapons aren't sharp enough, the tents aren't grand enough . . . even the ones who weren't behind the Quest before are enthusiastic now."

Newt snorted at that, sounding like one of his charges. Gerard grinned in agreement and then went on to say, "If nothing else, Morgain getting her fingers into the castle walls scared them that much. They think having the Grail will be some kind of magical talisman in and of itself, to keep her out and to keep Arthur safe."

"Isn't it?" Newt asked.

"No," Gerard said at the same time Ailis said, "yes."

"Well, which is it?" Newt asked.

"The Grail is magic, of a sort. Just like Morgain's tear or . . . or Merlin's staff, although he hardly ever uses it. It's where you store up power. Only . . ." Ailis slowed down, as though she were thinking her words through before uttering them.

Newt ceased grooming to listen. Gerard picked a bit of straw out of his pants leg with an expression of surprise. He was not accustomed to sitting on straw. It was sharper than he expected. Then again, not quite so uncomfortable as a troll's claws or a dragon's gaze. He still preferred a well-carved bench.

"Magic is power," Ailis went on. "It's not physical strength, but the ability to do, to create. The Grail is supposed to have that—the ability to create a High

King. So that's magic. Because the source of magic is belief. You know it exists, the way you know wind and rain are real. And so you trust in that belief. Merlin said that: You have to believe."

"The Grail is *more* than magic," Gerard said. "It's faith. Something you don't know and can't prove. You simply have to . . . have faith. And that's more powerful than anything Morgain might be able to create."

Newt made a noise in his throat that might have been a sign of dismay and turned back to grooming Loyal so as not to be drawn further into the discussion.

"You think so, do you?" Ailis's jaw had fallen open when Gerard had spoken, and she shut it now dramatically. "You, who were treating the Grail like a jousting trophy to be won by force of arms not a fortnight ago?"

Gerard had the decency to blush at that reminder. "Well, I'll have a chance to find out. Maybe." And now he was finally able to tell them what he had come to the stable to say in the first place. "Arthur has spoken. I'm to go with the knights on the Quest."

There was a stunned silence in the stable for a long moment, broken only by the sound of horses biting and chewing their grain. Then Newt smiled. "Haven't had enough racing about trying to be a hero?"

"Hardly a hero," Gerard replied. "I'm to be a servant of sorts myself. Fetch-and-carry mostly. I have a lot to learn," he said, far more humbly than the boy who had started out on a desperate journey weeks before. "Sir Rheynold says it will be years before I can become a knight, and years more after that before I'm ready to go challenge the dragon again."

"And win," Ailis said with confidence.

"And win," Newt agreed.

Gerard smiled, not with bravado but pleasure at the confidence his friends showed in him. "We'll see. First I have to make my name, somehow, on the Quest, and earn my spurs. Then we'll see about battling a dragon."

"Assuming it hasn't died of old age and boredom by then," Newt replied. "And don't expect me to carry your lance or saddle your horse for you, because I have no intention of waiting around that long to see you turn into a dragon-meal."

"You'll be coming with us then?" Gerard was grinning.

"We'll see," said Newt, picking up a wooden

comb and starting to brush out Loyal's mane. "If I've no other plans more interesting."

You'll have your own destiny, witch-child, a voice said softly in Ailis's head, even as she smiled at the now-familiar insults being tossed back and forth between the boys below her. *And you'll show them all what power the old magic can bring. . . .*

Ailis hushed the voice, but the echo of the words stayed deep within her. And now it bothered her slightly that she didn't know if the voice was Merlin's or Morgain's. There would be time enough for that later. When the Quest had gone off and Merlin had returned and the queen was paying less attention to what Ailis did and where she went. Gerard and Newt weren't the only ones who had plans for the future now.

Whatever would happen, it would be because Ailis decided it. She had sneaked out on this last adventure. Next time—and she doubted anything like *this* would ever happen again—she would be involved from the very beginning. She had earned that, more precious than fancy clothing or softer chores.

When Merlin came back, everything was going to change for her.

**THE ADVENTURE CONTINUES
IN GRAIL QUEST BOOK 2:**

MORGAIN'S
REVENGE

Gerard's steady walk down the hallway slowed,
almost without him noticing the change, and
his hand went to his waist where his sword was not
sheathed. No one carried a weapon inside Camelot's
walls unless they were on guard duty. But something
felt wrong, something that made him wish for solid
steel.

"You're getting as bad as Ailis, with her 'feelings,'"
he told himself. "You're inside the most secure place
on the entire island, surrounded by the finest warriors." *None of whom were able to prevent a spell from
being cast before.* His own thoughts worried at him.

There was nothing behind him, save a page dash-
ing on in another direction much farther down the
hallway, where it opened into an antechamber, and a
serving girl was gossiping with two guards. Light

from the wall lamps glinted off the pitcher she carried at her hip and off the metal of the guards' byrnies that covered them from shoulder to waist. He thought briefly about calling to alert the guards, but what would he say to them? "I felt a chill, an unease?" They would mock him, and rightfully so, when it turned out to be a door left open ahead, or something equally foolish. "And this from the squire the king so praised?" he could imagine them joking in their sleeping quarters.

No. He would say nothing. There was nothing to say.

Clenching his jaw and pushing his shoulders back into a square set, the way he'd seen Arthur do, he walked forward into the intersection where the hallway he was in met up with several others. A page was curled up on a windowsill, using the daylight to study a scroll of some sort. Two maids worked to take down a tapestry that hung on the opposite wall while a different tapestry waited, rolled on the floor, to replace it.

Gerard walked past them all, nodding to the page when the boy looked up from his reading to see who it was. He didn't know all the pages, but this one seemed to know him.

"Good morn, Ger!"

The voice was familiar, yes, but the boy's name escaped him totally, so Gerard merely raised a hand in greeting, and walked on. He was almost at his destination: through this antechamber, past the stairs that led to the cellars, and two doors down was the walkway to the guardroom, where the master of the guard would be found for receipt of Sir Rheynold's message. Same time spent getting back, even if he did pause at the kitchen, and he would probably arrive with the same argument he had left still going on.

"Months of boredom, followed by a mad dash across the marshes in the midst of the night," Gerard said out loud, quoting what his master had said years ago when describing the life of a knight. As a page he hadn't believed it, thinking that every moment of a knight's life must be excitement and derring-do.

He shivered again, a sudden ice-cold finger sliding down his spine in a deeply unpleasant way. Without thinking, he turned away from the hallway that led to his destination, and instead went left, finding himself running down one of the routes that servants used when they needed to move fast and stay out of sight.

Ailis had taught him about those ways, the semi-secret passages throughout Camelot that none of the nobles knew about. It had been a game when they were children, to race across the castle without using any of the main corridors or hallways. It had been years since he'd done that, but he didn't remember any of the passages having such a green cast to the stone, no matter what time of day or night.

Something is wrong. Something is very wrong, was all he had time to think before he turned a corner and was almost blinded by the intense green glow filling the passage.

Danger! His senses screamed at him, every muscle instinctively readying itself for combat, the way he had been trained to react. The glow burned, made him flinch away. *Magic! Danger!*

In the instant before his eyes shut in self-defense, his brain captured the image of Ailis, her hands reaching for him, her face terrified, as she was sucked backward into the heart of the glow.

Behind Ailis, her face the same diamond perfection he remembered from their last encounter—the sorceress Morgain!

"Ailis!" he shouted, fighting to move forward into the glow, reaching out for her, trying to find her. He had to save her! But even as he ran forward, something Newt had said during their adventure came back to him: *"Charging in blind's not the act of a hero, not if you don't know what's going on."*

It was just enough to make him hesitate, and then the glow was gone. The passageway was empty. No glow. No Morgain. No Ailis.

Gerard stared for a moment in disbelief. How? How did Morgain get in here? And what was Ailis doing with her?

Gerard scanned the space again, as though hoping that Ailis would reappear out of thin air or that his eyes had been playing tricks on him.

But the hallway remained empty. With a curse, Gerard turned on his heels and ran for the Council Room.

Newt was right. As much as he'd wanted to follow Ailis into that glow, it would have been the act of a fool. Morgain was dangerous. This was a matter for older, wiser, more experienced men. Ailis's life—and the security of Camelot—depended on it!